Slocum's Sixth Sense

Slocum started to turn to face the danger he felt behind him when something hard rammed him in the small of his back.

A thousand thoughts coursed through his brain at that moment with blinding speed and none of them made any sense.

"Mister, you even twitch and I'll blow a hole in you big enough to drive a wagon through."

Slocum froze and waited for the hammer to drop, for the sound of the explosion that would blot out all his senses and plunge his mortal self into the final everlasting abyss of death . . .

JAKE LOGAN

SLOCUM
AND THE SOCORRO
SALOON SIRENS

JOVE BOOKS, NEW YORK

THE BERKLEY PUBLISHING GROUP
Published by the Penguin Group
Penguin Group (USA) Inc.
375 Hudson Street, New York, New York 10014, USA
Penguin Group (Canada), 90 Eglinton Avenue East, Suite 700, Toronto, Ontario M4P 2Y3, Canada
(a division of Pearson Penguin Canada Inc.)
Penguin Books Ltd., 80 Strand, London WC2R 0RL, England
Penguin Group Ireland, 25 St. Stephen's Green, Dublin 2, Ireland (a division of Penguin Books Ltd.)
Penguin Group (Australia), 250 Camberwell Road, Camberwell, Victoria 3124, Australia
(a division of Pearson Australia Group Pty. Ltd.)
Penguin Books India Pvt. Ltd., 11 Community Centre, Panchsheel Park, New Delhi—110 017, India
Penguin Group (NZ), 67 Apollo Drive, Rosedale, Auckland 0632, New Zealand
(a division of Pearson New Zealand Ltd.)
Penguin Books (South Africa) (Pty.) Ltd., 24 Sturdee Avenue, Rosebank, Johannesburg 2196,
South Africa

Penguin Books Ltd., Registered Offices: 80 Strand, London WC2R 0RL, England

This is a work of fiction. Names, characters, places, and incidents either are the product of the author's imagination or are used fictitiously, and any resemblance to actual persons, living or dead, business establishments, events, or locales is entirely coincidental.

SLOCUM AND THE SOCORRO SALOON SIRENS

A Jove Book / published by arrangement with the author

PRINTING HISTORY
Jove edition / October 2011

ISBN: 978-0-515-15001-8

JOVE®
Jove Books are published by The Berkley Publishing Group,
a division of Penguin Group (USA) Inc.,
375 Hudson Street, New York, New York 10014.
JOVE® is a registered trademark of Penguin Group (USA) Inc.
The "J" design is a trademark of Penguin Group (USA) Inc.

PRINTED IN THE UNITED STATES OF AMERICA

10 9 8 7 6 5 4 3 2 1

1

The old blind horse followed the man on the black. It dragged one foot on the dusty, rocky road, favored the lame hind leg. Its once-sorrel hide was flecked with gray, and there were leathery sores on its shoulders and back. It wore a hemp halter that was frayed and worn from years of use. Its ribs showed through its withered, moth-eaten hide. It seemed to know by the looks of its skeletal frame and blind white eyes that it was making its last journey. The horse seemed to know that it was soon to die.

When John Slocum left Fort Craig that morning, he headed north toward Albuquerque, another contract in his saddlebags. He had just delivered a dozen horses he'd driven up from Las Cruces three days before, and not only was the Army satisfied with the horses, but they'd asked for a dozen more. And Slocum knew just where to get them, from a rancher he knew who owned a horse ranch in Cedar Crest.

The blind horse, he knew, was called Moses, and like its

1

namesake, it would never see the promised land. John's mind went back to that morning when he was saddling up Ferro to leave the fort. Jimmy Calderon, the sergeant wrangler, had come up to him in the stall.

"John, will you do me a favor?" Jimmy had asked. "A big favor."

"Depends, Jimmy. Is it legal?"

Jimmy had not laughed.

"It is a serious favor. Did you see that old blind horse out in the corral, standing against the fence?"

"I saw it. It looks like it's on its last legs."

"I am supposed to kill old Moses, but I can't. That horse is almost fourteen years old and went blind two years ago."

"Just put it down, Jimmy. One shot to the brain."

"I cannot do that, John. Moses was with the Seventh Cavalry when Custer was massacred. I think one of Benteen's men rode him. He wound up here at Fort Craig and I took care of him. He had wounds in him from Sioux arrows. He became the mount of a cavalry officer who truly loved the horse. But he was killed by Apaches, and Moses limped back to the post. Just like a faithful old dog."

"What is it you want from me, Jimmy?"

"I want you to take Moses with you and, well, put him down someplace where he does not know nobody. Someplace quiet where he can hear the doves and maybe hear quail calling in the desert. Put him on a little hill with the yucca and the prickly pear, the nopal and the cholla. He has suffered so much. I can no longer see him to suffer."

"I don't like to shoot a horse, Jimmy. It's as bad as killing a man."

"I know. I will pay you five dollars to do this for me."

Slocum shook his head.

"I wouldn't take money for a thing like that."

"I will pay for the bullet."

"No, Jimmy. I can't take blood money. But I will take the horse with me, and when I find a good place for him to die, I'll put him to sleep."

Calderon did not smile, but he got the old halter out of the tack room and harnessed the old horse. He put his arms around Moses's neck and said good-bye in Spanish. There were tears in Jimmy's eyes when he handed the halter rope to Slocum.

Slocum looked back at the horse. It hurt to look at him with his blind eyes and ravaged hide, the ribs presaging the skeleton he would soon become. He could almost feel the horse's pain, but could not understand the animal's resignation. He had once been a proud horse, a cavalry horse, and he had seen men die and horses flail the air with their hooves when they were shot down by Sioux or Cheyenne.

Now, he rode the ochre road north through a desolate landscape broken only by rocks, cactus, and yucca, as barren, almost, as the *Jornada del Muerte*, the Journey of Death that had claimed so many lives since the white man had ventured westward. And this place, beyond the *Jornada*, was just as bleak and unforgiving as Death Valley in California.

The morning cool dissipated under the yellow glare of the boiling sun. It hung in the sky like a shimmering disk of hammered armor plucked from a cauldron filled with molten gold. Long, thin streamers of clouds floated in white plumes across the blue expanse of the tranquil sky.

Suddenly, Slocum's gaze was broken by the sight of a woman stumbling toward him through islands of stone and prickly pear. Her stringy auburn hair looked damp and her blue eyes were wide with a look that made Slocum think of panic, or fear.

"Mister, mister, can you help me?" the woman sobbed. "My father. He—he's hurt. Hurt bad."

She stopped short of the road. She wrung her hands. Slocum looked at her smudged face, the dark lines of tears that had loosened the kohl of her eyelashes. Her dress was flocked with dirt as if she had been dragged through the sand and dirt of the desert. It was wrinkled and torn so that patches of her skirt showed through the faded green fabric.

"Where is he?"

"Just up there, under that little knoll," she said. "Please hurry. Do you have water?"

"Yes," he said.

She turned and ran back through the cactus as if she were rushing through dandelions, unmindful of the spines on the prickly pear or the delicate razor-sharp lace of the cholla. He turned Ferro and let the horse pick his way through the rocks and the cactus. The young woman was no longer visible, but he heard moaning and her soft soothing voice.

A man lay in a concave depression just below the knoll. He had no hat and his face was burned to a rosy hue by exposure to the sun. His jaw was stenciled with beard stubble, his lips dry and cracked. He looked emaciated in his torn shirt, his filthy denims. His boots were scarred by rocks and thorns, his clothing embedded with desert soil.

Slocum swung down out of the saddle and ground-tied Ferro and Moses to a small creosote bush. He unslung a full canteen from the saddle horn and carried it to the sprawled-out man, whose dark eyes were wet and wide with pain.

The man stared up at Slocum with glazed eyes. Slocum uncorked his canteen and put the spout to the man's lips.

"Just a taste," he said. "You look too dry to take more than a sip."

Water trickled from the canteen over the man's lips and into his mouth.

The woman gasped and squatted next to Slocum. She

touched a hand to her father's feverish face. The man gurgled as some of the water slid down his throat. He coughed and spat out a few droplets. Slocum took the canteen away and corked it.

Then he looked at the man's hands. The fingertips were all blackened and he could see small red rivulets under the skin and nails.

"What happened to him?" he asked the woman.

"They—They tortured him," she said. "There are cuts all over his chest."

"They?"

"It's a long story," she said. "I helped my father escape, but . . ."

"But what?" Slocum asked.

"If they find him, they'll kill him."

"What's your name?" Slocum asked. He realized that the woman was on the verge of hysteria. She looked ready to fall into a swoon.

She stared at him, as if she hadn't expected the question.

"I'm Penelope Swain," she said. "My pa's name is Jethro. Jethro Swain. Oh, mister, will you help us?"

"Where were you going?" he asked.

"I don't know. We just had to get away from that awful place. Maybe to Fort Craig?"

"That's a long walk from here."

"I'd like to take him to his brother's, but that's a far piece, too."

"If you'll show me the way, I'll take you and your father to his brother's. What's his name?"

"Obadiah Swain. My Uncle Obie. That's what we call him."

"Does your uncle know about your father?"

"No, not yet. I think they tortured my pa to find out where he lives, where he has his cache of silver."

"So, this is about money?"

"Silver, yes."

"This man, your father, needs a doctor."

"I'm a nurse. I can tend to him if we can get him to a safe place."

"I can carry your father double on my horse. You can ride the other bareback."

She looked over at the two horses.

"That horse looks blind," she said. "And it's crippled, isn't it?"

"Yes, the horse is blind and lame." He did not tell her that he was going to put the horse down. For now, Moses would serve to carry her on its back, while he carried her father on Ferro. "Before we go, Penelope—"

"Call me Penny," she interrupted him. "And what's your name?"

"John Slocum," he answered. "Before we go, Penny, you'd better tell me what I'm up against. Who tortured your father and who wants to get your uncle's silver?"

"I don't know who carried my pa off in the middle of the night, nor who tortured him. But I do know where they were holding him."

"That might help. Where?"

"Socorro," she said. "The Socorro Saloon."

"Socorro? That mean's 'help' in Spanish. I've never been there."

"Yes, the word means 'help,' or 'aid,' but that saloon is an evil place. My pa isn't the only one they kidnapped and tortured. And I know some of the men were killed, murdered by those vultures."

"Vultures don't murder anything," he said.

"These vultures at the Socorro Saloon do."

Slocum drew a breath. He gave Jethro another taste of water and handed his canteen to Penny.

"See if you can get on that old horse," he said. "I'll take care of your pa."

Slocum lifted Jethro up and felt a wetness at the back of his shirt.

When he looked down at his hand, it was covered with fresh blood.

2

"Where are we going?" Slocum asked Penny once they were mounted.

She pointed across the river to a distant point that was meaningless to Slocum.

"How did you and your father get across the river?" he asked.

"I'll show you," she said.

The Rio Grande del Norte was a formidable river, wide and deep. As they left the road and angled toward it, he could hear the soft moan of its waters, and when he saw it up close, sunlight glinted off the brown and faint green of its glassy surface. Penny pointed to two rocks a short distance upriver, small boulders that marked a place where the river slowed at a bend and there were sandy islands breaking up the flow. On the other side, there were two more small boulders.

"That's the ford," Penny said.

"How deep is the deepest part?" he asked.

"Pa and I waded it," she said. "In the deep part it came up to our waists. The bottom is solid there."

"Let me know if I get off track," he said, and pulled on the halter rope to shorten it. As Ferro stepped into the stream, Moses followed, his blind eyes oblivious to the danger, but his nostrils turned rubbery as he sniffed the river waters and followed Slocum. The water came up to Ferro's chest in the deepest part. Slocum lifted his stovepipe boots out of the stirrups to keep them dry.

They reached the other side in less than ten minutes. They came out right next to the two stones that marked the ford.

"You went across perfect," Penny said. "Now don't follow that trail. It leads to Socorro, and we don't want to go there."

"As you say," he said. "I wonder if your father's kidnappers are still looking for him?"

"I don't know," she said. "But they might be. Just ride off to the right about a half mile and then go straight toward the mountains."

There was a thin blue break on the distant horizon, and he could see white mountain peaks gleaming in the sun.

He went where she told him to go, and the land seemed to grow more desolate and lifeless the farther they got off the trail. Lizards blinked as they rested on rocks, and he heard a rattlesnake shake its tail in a clump of prickly pear. A quail sat atop a distant yucca and sounded a warning before it took flight and disappeared.

Slocum learned a great deal from Penny as they rode through the bleak, trackless desert, well off the road. He learned a lot, but not enough. She seemed reluctant to tell him too much, or else, he figured, she did not trust him. But as she talked, he tried to form pictures in his mind, not only of her father's ordeal, but of his addiction to opium, and the mysterious Socorro Saloon.

He did not want to tell her that he thought her father was dying, even as he held him tight against his chest, blood seeping onto Slocum's black shirt.

"Can you tell me how your father wound up in this condition?" Slocum asked.

"I don't know all of it. Some men came into our house. They had guns and their faces were covered. They dragged my father out of bed and took him away. I didn't find out where my pa was until yesterday."

"Is that where we're going now?" Slocum asked. "To your house?"

"Yes. That's where I keep my medicines. I know Pa is in serious condition. I'm going to try and save his life."

"Shouldn't you take him to a doctor?"

Penny made a sound in her throat that came out through her nostrils. It sounded like an airy snort.

"A doctor would just tell me what to do. I already know what to do."

"You do?"

"I think so. Please, no more questions. I don't want to think about Pa just now."

"Well, he's bleeding," Slocum said. "I think he might have a back wound."

"Bleeding a little is probably the best thing for him right now, Mr. Slocum."

The ground rose beneath them, rising above the level where they had been. They rode through flowered yucca, prickly pear, ocotillo, sage, and scrub juniper, the stately forms of saguaro standing like sentinels over a barren land, hoarding water in their trunks, protecting their treasure with sharp spines.

Something off to the left caught Slocum's eyes, and he turned his head. Sunlight splashed on whitewashed adobe walls and a rusted cistern on wooden stilts.

"That's Socorro," Penny said.

There were scattered adobes, small earthen dwellings that seemed to have been placed there at random. There was a three-story building that looked like an old fort, surrounded by smaller ones that were one and two stories high, with log ends jutting from the inner ceilings.

"That big building is the main hotel," she said. "Next to it is the Socorro Saloon, where Pa was held prisoner. It has a basement, one of the few in Socorro." She seemed to shiver as she spoke, with either fear or revulsion, Slocum couldn't tell which.

"Not much of a town."

"It was built long ago as a haven for those who managed to survive the *Jornada del Muerto*," she said.

"The Journey of Death."

"Yes. That's why it's named Socorro."

That's when Slocum saw the sloping plain north of the town. It was littered with little white slabs of wood, crosses, headstones, and a profusion of flowers tied together in bundles or fashioned into wreaths. It was the cemetery, Slocum knew, a place where men, women, and children were buried, and likely where the man in the saddle with him would end up. The name of the town, then, was more than a little ironic, considering the number of graves on Boot Hill.

"It wasn't any help to your father."

"No. The saloon is an evil place. Please, Mr. Slocum, we must ride on, get out of sight of the village. I don't trust those people."

"All the people?" he asked.

"Those who might be watching," she said, and he heard the faint tremor in her voice. They rode on, out of sight of Socorro.

"Do we have far to go?" he asked. The blind horse was stumbling and kept pulling against the lead rope as if it wanted to return to the fort and lie down. Its white eyes were a constant reminder of its blindness and its gray-streaked hide a reminder of its age.

"Three or four miles," she said.

Beyond the town of Socorro, Slocum saw the rippling waters of a mirage, streaks of vaporous silver that glistened in the sun, vanishing and reappearing like the ghost of a lake, the ghosts of shining streams. He shifted his glance to the land around them, and soon the town and the cemetery had vanished like the watery mirage. The sun scorched the already burnt land, and he wiped sweat from his brow with the bandanna around his neck. Penny rode straight-backed, like a princess on a fine steed, and he marveled at the way she held herself in such heat and under such circumstances.

It seemed more like five miles to Slocum before Penny pointed to a low adobe building nestled between two small hillocks. But the dwelling was on high ground, compared to its surroundings, and as they rode closer, Slocum saw that the two hillocks were braced by deep channels cut into the earth, both leading to a wide, rocky plain.

"That's where we live," Penny said.

"Pretty smart of your pa to cut those ditches on either side of those little hills," Slocum said.

"We get a lot of flash floods out here," she said. "Pa dug those canals so that the water, when we get a big rain, just drains off down onto that flat."

"Like I said, pretty smart," Slocum said.

"Pa is a smart man," she said, "in most things."

Slocum resisted the urge to ask her about those things he wasn't so smart about, but they rode up to the hitch rail, and a black-and-white dog rushed out to greet them, its tail flicking back and forth in a wild semaphoric pleasure.

"That's Daisy," Penny said. "She's a border collie. She won't bite you."

Penny tied the halter rope to the hitch rail in front of the adobe house and walked around to the side of Slocum's horse. He stepped out of the saddle with care. He let the wounded man tilt toward him, then pulled him down. Penny took her father in her arms.

"I can take it from here," she said. "There's a lean-to and a corral out back where you can put the horses up. You can grain and water them there."

"You don't need any help getting your pa inside the house?"

"John, I'm used to caring for the sick and the lame," she said, and he thought he detected a slight note of sarcasm in her voice. She put one of her father's arms over her shoulder and walked him to the front door. She went inside and Slocum walked the horses around the adobe.

Out back, there was, as she had said, a pole corral, a large lean-to where a horse and a mule stood under the canopy in the shade. He turned Ferro and Moses into the corral, stripped his saddle and bridle off Ferro. There was a water trough under the lean-to, and a bin full of hay sticking through the slats. Room enough for a horse's or a mule's head between the boards. Well built, he thought, all of it. The corral, the lean-to, the adobe house, which blended into the landscape so well, he knew it would be invisible at a distance.

He walked around to the front of the house and stared at a mirage that bristled on the horizon less than a mile away. He saw movement inside the tilting mirror of silvery waters and shaded his eyes with his hands. Sweat trickled down the back of his neck and streamed along his spine. The hairs on the back of his neck stiffened and began to tingle.

Two riders seemed to wade through the watery mirage, their shapes distorted and ghostly, as if they were the dead rising from a desert lake.

He set his rifle and scabbard down and waited as the riders left the mirage in their wake and continued their steady pace straight toward him.

Slocum patted the belly gun he kept inside his belt and lifted his .45 Colt an inch out of its holster, then let it slide back so that it was loose, but ready to draw at a second's notice.

One man was taller than the other, and older. The younger one was wild-eyed and nervous, with hair poking out from under his hat like straw. The older man was lean, whiplash thin, with a shadow of beard stubble flocking his chin. He was the one who spoke first as the two men halted a few yards from Slocum, their eyes fixed on him as if he were an escaped convict in prison stripes.

"Howdy, stranger," the tall man said. "You got business hereabouts?"

"If I do," Slocum said, "it's my business."

"Maybe not."

"Oh?" Slocum said.

The younger man looked as if he were all wound up with coils of springy wire and was about to explode into a dozen pieces.

"Wasn't that Swain and his daughter you rode up with a few minutes ago?" The tall man's eyes were like twin gun barrels, dark, ominous, unflinching.

"Might have been," Slocum said. "So what?"

"So, you're steppin' into something that ain't none of your business."

"Let's blow this jasper plumb to hell," the young man said, his blue eyes full of sunlight that shot spears at Slocum.

"Steady, Roger," the tall man said.

"Come on, Morg. We can take him."

Slocum braced himself. The towheaded young man was arching his hand just above the pistol hanging at his hip.

"Let's give the man a chance," Morg said. "He ain't got no business here, and he probably just wants a drink of cool water afore he is off, back to where he come from."

"Seems to me, you two are the trespassers here," Slocum said. "I was invited."

The man called Morg scowled, and the expression on his face changed in an instant.

But Slocum had his eye on the towhead named Roger, whose springs were ready to uncoil.

"Shit," Roger said, and his hand dove for the butt of his pistol.

Slocum went into a crouch and drew his pistol so fast, it was a blur in his hand.

Roger pulled his pistol free of its holster. Almost. The pistol had not quite cleared leather when Slocum hammered back, aimed, and fired. His pistol bucked in his hand and he swung it on Morg as his bullet plowed into Roger's gut with a sound like a heavy slap.

Roger let out a grunt and his hand went limp. His pistol slid from numb fingers and spanged on the rocky ground.

Morg stiffened, but kept both hands in sight as Slocum's pistol barrel settled on a line of sight straight to his chest.

"You want to eat some lead, too, mister?" Slocum said.

Roger groaned. He teetered in his saddle, but held on. He clutched his stomach, and his fingers ran with red blood.

"God, Morg," Roger gasped, "it hurts real bad."

"You won this one, stranger," Morg said, "but if you come to Socorro, we'll meet again."

Morg grabbed the reins of Roger's horse and turned around.

The two rode off as Penny emerged from the house, her face flushed, bathed in sweat, her eyes wide as an owl's.

"John," she said as she rushed up to him, "what have you done?"

"Those two," he said. "I shot one of them."

"Do you know who they were?" she asked.

"I haven't the least idea of who they were. The young one was a hothead and he drew down on me. I shot him in the belly."

"That was Roger Degnan," she said. "His brother, Patrick, is the sheriff of Socorro."

"Know who the other man is? The kid called him Morg."

Penny shivered against him.

"That's Morgan Sombra. The people in town call him Shadow. He's a mestizo who works at the saloon. John, he's a gunman. A killer."

"A killer, eh? Well, he must be off duty today."

"Come on inside," she said. "John, you're in grave danger now."

"From those two?"

"From the same bunch who kidnapped and tortured my father. Oh, what have I done? I fear you'll be killed. All on my account."

They entered the house. It was cool and smelled of mint and wisteria blossoms. Slocum slid his pistol back in its holster. He would reload it after he had a sip of the tea in the glass Penny handed him.

She led him to a chair in the front room. He sat down.

"Penny," he said. "Those two men were no different from many others I've run into out West. Don't you worry yourself none about me. How's your pa?"

To his surprise, she leaned down and kissed him on the forehead. Then she flitted away and disappeared down the hall. He thought he could smell alcohol and some kind of medicine. He drank the cool tea as that fleeting kiss burned on his forehead.

3

Slocum ejected the empty hull from his pistol and pulled a bullet from his gun belt. He slid the cartridge into the empty chamber, then fished out a cheroot from his pocket. There was a clay *cenicero* on the little table next to the divan. He lit the cheroot and put the dead match into the ashtray.

He looked at his pistol before he slid it back in his holster. That's when the thought occurred to him. He got up and walked outside, strode to where Roger had dropped his pistol. He picked it up and dusted it off with his hand, carried it back into the house.

He sat down and examined the pistol. A wry smile curved on his lips. The pistol was a converted Remington New Model Army .36 caliber. It had a wooden grip and the straps were brass. He had carried such a pistol in the war, when it was cap and ball. This one now had become a percussion model and the cylinder was filled with brass cartridges. He laid it on the table and puffed on his cheroot as he looked around the room.

The furnishings were Spartan, but colorful. The chairs were made from nail kegs with stuffed deer hides for cushioning. There was a rainbow-weave serape draping another chair, which was fashioned from sturdy oak and the wood polished to a high sheen. Flowers jutted from earthen vases lacquered with vivid colors. The walls were bare but painted a soft lavender with green trim at the ceiling and floorboards. The sofa on which he sat was sturdy and comfortable, well cushioned with stuffed woolen cloth. He tapped ashes into the *cenicero* and listened to the noises coming from another room, the tinkle of bottles and the clink of metal, footsteps, and guttural sounds he assumed were made by Penny's father, Jethro Swain.

A few minutes later, Penny appeared in the doorway.

"John," she said, "come with me. I want you to see what they did to my father."

He got up and mashed his cheroot in the ashtray. He followed her down a hall and into a bedroom. The room was windowless and the bed, just large enough for one person, stood waist high. There were open cabinets with apothecary bottles, salves, unguents, and flasks filled with various colored liquids. It smelled like a hospital or a field infirmary, with the pungent aroma of alcohol and other medicants burning his nostrils. She had lit lamps in front of a large mirror on the dresser that was slanted so that the reflected light shone on the bed.

Jethro lay on his back, naked except for his shorts. His eyes were closed, but he looked at peace, with no sign of the pain that must have been coursing through his body.

"See what they did to Pa," she whispered.

"Is he asleep?"

"I gave him laudanum. I sewed up a wound in his back. Luckily, it didn't puncture his lung, but he lost a great deal of blood."

Slocum walked close to the edge of the bed and looked at the marks on Jethro's body. There were dark smudges that looked like burn marks on his legs and arms, his chest and neck.

"Cigarettes," he said.

"The larger ones were made from cigars. They tortured him, John. Look at the soles of his feet."

Slocum bent down and looked. There were striped scars on his heels and pads.

"A hot poker, I think," she said. "Red hot." She winced as she said it.

Slocum stood up straight.

"Why were they torturing him?" he asked.

"It's a long story."

"I've got time. Is your pa going to be all right?"

"They fed him opium and I gave him laudanum, so I don't know about his mind or his addiction. But his body will heal."

"They wanted something from him," Slocum said. "Information?"

"Yes. Oddly enough, I think the opium helped Pa withstand the torture."

"What did they want from him?"

He looked up at her when she didn't answer right away.

She worried her lower lip as if deciding how much she should tell the man in black who was, after all, a stranger. Perhaps a Good Samaritan, but not someone she knew well, or could trust.

"You don't have to tell me, Penny," he said. "None of my business. But from the looks of your pa, they worked him over pretty damned good. I'd hate to think they tortured him just because they didn't like him."

"They wanted something from him," she said, her voice soft and barely audible. "And knowing my father, I don't believe he told them what they wanted to know. I know he wouldn't. He had too much respect."

"Respect?"

"Yes. For—for his brother, my uncle."

He started to walk out of the room.

"Wait," she said. "You helped us. You deserve to know. I think you do. It—It's just that I don't know who you are, or even if I can trust you. I hope you understand."

"Best keep those reasons to yourself, Penny," he said. "You don't owe me anything. And you're right. You don't know me."

"Who are you?" she said, and then put her hand over her mouth as if to stifle anything else she might say.

"Nobody. I'm just a drifter. I am like the wayward wind, the tumbleweed, the little dust devil that blows across the prairie and then disappears."

"Do you have a home, or a ranch? Where did you come from?"

"The land is my home. The sky my roof, the streams my well, the woods my larder, the campfire my kitchen. I need nothing else. The West is my home and I roam it at will, beholden to no man, with only my own mouth to feed."

"You don't look like a drifter. Are you wanted by the law?"

"Wanted?"

"I saw you shoot Roger. You were very fast on the draw. Are you a gunman?"

"I feel like I'm being questioned by someone with a badge right now. I don't think of myself as a gunman, although it is a tool I use when the situation calls for it. I don't like killing a man, but sometimes, in this life, it's a matter of survival. I aim to survive for as long as I can."

She looked him up and down, at the flat-crowned black hat, the black shirt, the gun belt bristling with cartridges, the revolver, the black pants, and the stovepipe boots. She looked at him and sighed in resignation.

"Very well. It's my Uncle Obie, Obadiah. There's something funny about that Socorro Saloon. They know Uncle Obie has been mining silver, but they don't know where his mines are. What's more, they know he's not just taking out ore and taking it to the refinery in Albuquerque, he's smelting it himself. They tried to get Pa to tell them where Uncle Obie lives and where his mines are."

"So they can steal his silver."

"Exactly. Pa would never tell them where Obie lives."

"But those jaspers at the saloon must be searching far and wide for those mines."

"They are. But Obie's house is well hidden, and fortified. He has men working for him who are armed and would shoot any intruder. Uncle Obie's a very private person, almost like a hermit."

"But he can't hide from those thieves forever," Slocum said. "Eventually, they'll find out where he lives."

"Maybe. But I doubt they would find any of his mines. Uncle Obie keeps them well hidden."

"Anything can be found," Slocum said. "It's just a question of time. Meanwhile, I think your uncle is in danger. Does he know about the men who are looking for him? Does he know what they did to his brother?"

Penny shook her head.

"No, he doesn't," she said. "He doesn't come here often and I'm afraid to ride out to tell him. I'm afraid someone might follow me."

"That's a possibility," Slocum said. "Would you trust me to talk to your uncle and tell him about Jethro?"

"Let's go into the front room," she said. "Pa can probably hear us, although he seems to be unconscious."

"Sure," Slocum said. He followed her into the front

room. She sat in a chair and waved him to the sofa. He sat down.

"It's not that I don't trust you," she said, "but Uncle Obie is due to stop by at any time. In fact, I expected him yesterday. I'd rather wait until he shows up. He's very careful. He never rides the same trail to our house, and he always comes at night."

"I see," Slocum said. "Sure, whatever you think is best. Maybe I'd best be on my way. I was headed for Albuquerque to look at some horses that I might resell to the Army at Fort Craig."

"Is it urgent?" she asked. She sat there so prim and reserved, literally on the edge of her seat, that he thought she might sprout wings and fly away like a bird at any moment. He realized that she was scared and still worried about her father.

"No, I don't have a timetable," he said. "But you probably don't want a stranger hanging around."

"You have a bedroll," she said. "And I've loads of soft pillows. If you don't mind sleeping on the floor, I'd like you to stay until Uncle Obie shows up. It could be tonight or tomorrow night."

"Or next week," he said, so quickly he regretted it. He saw her stiffen and slide back in her chair as if he had punched her.

"No. If it's more than three days, you're free to go. I—I just feel safer with you here, and my father does need tending."

"You don't have to go to work in town?"

"No. I told the doctor I'd be away for a few days. There's another nurse. They can manage without me."

"I'll stay, then," he said. "But . . ."

"But what?" she said.

"It might not look good."

"To whom? The town doesn't care. I have no close friends. It's been just Pa and me and his brother. I don't care what people say."

He knew he liked her then, for what she had said, for what she was.

A ray of sunlight fell on her face and made it shine with a golden radiance. At that moment, he would have laid down his life for her.

"I'll fix you a nice supper," she said.

"Obliged."

"Oh, you don't have to feel obligated. I have to eat and maybe I can pour some soup into Pa. He's thin as a rail."

"If I can be of any help in tending to him, you just let me know," he said.

"Why, thank you. I'll surely call on you if need be."

He looked at her and shook his head.

"What?" she said.

"Oh, nothing. I was just thinking how unfair life can be. In your case, you seem to have run into a stretch of bad luck. It's sad, that's all."

"You're a very compassionate man, John Slocum. I feel lucky to have met you."

He didn't know what to say, but he felt a warmth suffuse his flesh and it had nothing to do with the sunlight that sprayed the room, soaking up some of the coolness. It had to do with the sincerity of her words and the beauty of her nature.

Penny, he decided, was a woman to ride the river with. Any river. Anywhere on earth.

She left him, then, to tend to her father, and Slocum walked outside and around the house to get his bedroll.

For the first time in many months, he felt at home.

4

Slocum watched the way Penny served their supper. Each dish she laid down on the table seemed special. She moved with grace and poise through the shadows and the candlelight, like a dancer making entrances and exits on a lighted stage.

When she sat down opposite him, she smiled.

"There," she said. "Now we can eat."

She bowed her head and brought her hands together in an attitude of prayer. Her lips did not move and she made no sound. Slocum sat frozen until she had finished saying silent grace.

The sun was setting and Penny had lit two candles on the table. Lamps glowed on other tables and shelves, their light mingling with the last radiance of the sun as it splashed through the open windows and painted the adobe walls.

"How's your pa doing?" Slocum asked.

"Sleeping. I gave him more laudanum. Sleep is a powerful curative."

She opened a pot and forked meat onto Slocum's plate. The smell was delicious.

"Lamb?" he said.

She laughed. "Yes, lamb chops. Uncle Obie gets them from a Basque who raises sheep in the foothills. I have a springhouse, which you haven't seen. The meat cures out there and stays cool from a spring seep."

She set boiled new potatoes on his plate, and scooped up a small pile of green succulents cut into cubes.

"What are those?" he asked.

She laughed and dipped some onto her own plate.

"Try them, and then I'll tell you," she said.

Slocum spooned a few cubes into his mouth, chewed them.

"Very tasty," he said. "I'm still mystified, though."

"The Mexicans call them *nopalitos tiernos*," she said. "They take the young prickly pear cactus, remove the spines from them, and dice the cactus. They're very good in chili, and I keep them in glass airtights."

"In the springhouse," he said, and they both laughed.

"Yes. It's quite deep, like a cellar, and is naturally cooled by the seeping spring."

He cut a chunk of lamb and forked it into his mouth.

"The food is delicious," he said. "You're a fine cook."

"My uncle said that if I ever gave up nursing, he would hire me as a cook. I try to keep it a secret from everyone else."

The candlelight softened her features and hollowed out her eyes with shadows except when she lifted her head to look at him. Then, her eyes shone like star sapphires, blue as an April sky.

Toward the end of the meal, Slocum felt something brush against his boot. He ignored it, until it began to travel up to his trousered leg. He reached down and touched a bare foot.

Toes kneaded his trousers and pressed against the flesh of his leg.

She looked at him and smiled, her eyes hollow with shadow, invisible. Her laugh was soft and merry as a child's.

"Are you flirting with me, Penny?" he asked.

"A little," she said. "I didn't realize how lonely it was out here until Pa was kidnapped and until you came here. Forgive me for being so forward."

"Nothing to forgive, Penny. Everyone gets lonely."

"I've had my schooling and my work. I never lacked friends. Until we came here. To this godforsaken place."

"Why don't you move into town?"

She made a guttural sound of disgust.

"Ugggh. I've seen the men and women of Socorro. No thanks."

"But you work there."

"I didn't for a long time. Until Pa scolded me. He said I was driving him crazy with my knitting, sewing, trying to garden on land that will only grow gourds and weeds. I had a nursing degree, and there was a clinic in town. I ride there every morning and come home at night so tired I can't think."

"But you like nursing," he said. It wasn't a question.

"I love it. But it's very demanding and leaves no time for . . . for other pursuits, and besides, the men and women who have approached me, I find revolting."

"That's too bad," he said. "And sad."

"Yes, it's sad, and I'm acting foolish. But I've never met anyone like you, John. Not in nursing school back in Nashville, or out here."

"How was your pa kidnapped?" he said, to change the subject. He did not want to hear her life story. Not just yet.

"The Socorro Saloon employs glitter gals, women of ill repute, ladies of the night, whatever you want to call them. Pa met one of the girls who worked there and started sparking her. She lured him there, if you ask me, like a modern-day Siren."

"One of the glitter gals?"

"I'm not sure. I know he met Maria Luisa Echeverria at the Socorro Saloon. She was poor and he felt sorry for her. She was much younger than Pa, and I think her mother was a glitter gal, a woman named Miranda. Pa wanted to marry Maria Luisa, and she told him he would have to ask permission from her mother. When he went there to the saloon one night, he was overpowered by some men and never came back home."

"Did Maria Luisa know he was going to be kidnapped?"

"I don't know. Probably. Certainly Miranda did. She's a witch."

"You met her?"

"At the clinic. John, this is all very depressing to think about."

"Sorry," he said.

Penny withdrew her foot, then touched him again with her patty-toed caresses as they both finished up their meals.

"I'll clear up the dishes," she said. "Why don't you smoke one of those cheroots in the front room and I'll join you when I finish. Would you like some brandy?"

"No thanks," he said. "I have a bottle of Kentucky bourbon in my saddlebag. I might have a taste of that."

"Maybe I'd like a taste of that, myself," she said.

"I'd be pleasured if you would."

She smiled at him as he arose from the table. He smiled back and walked into the front room.

He was just lighting up when Penny appeared with two small glasses and set them on the little table in front of the sofa.

"For the drinks," she said. "Do you want a glass of water?"

"No. I drink it straight."

When she went back to the kitchen, he dug out his bottle of bourbon and set it on the table with the two glasses. He smoked his cheroot down to the size of a fingertip and put it out in the ashtray.

The sky outside glowed with a flaming sunset and he heard the distant yaps of coyotes and the sizzle of insects. The lamp made the room dance with shadows and sprayed a warm glow on the polished tables and chairs. It was quiet when Penny entered the room. She was wearing a filmy blue nightgown that reflected the color of her eyes. The gown clung to her lithe form and he realized it was made of silk. When she sat down, he saw the flash of her bare legs and felt a tug of desire in his loins.

He poured bourbon in both glasses. She looked at his bedroll all laid out against the wall in one corner of the room.

She took the drink he handed her.

"Shall we clink glasses?" she said.

"Only if there's a toast to give."

"I have one," she said, a slight smile carving her lips into a curve. "To a wonderful friendship."

She touched her glass to his and it made a soft clink.

"Long may it last," he said.

She sipped her drink. He swallowed a mouthful. It went down smooth and warm.

"Very nice," she said, and glanced at his bedroll again.

"This floor is so hard," she said. "Are you sure you don't want to sleep on the soft sofa?"

"No, the floor is fine. I would have slept on hard ground tonight if I hadn't met you."

"I have a soft bed," she said. "Big enough for two."

"Are you offering me something?" he asked, fixing her with a bold stare, his eyes like obsidian flint.

"You are young and handsome. I am single, and so are you."

"Are you sure?" he asked.

"Sure of what? Myself? No. Of you, yes. There is something about you that I find appealing. Attractive, too. Your manliness. I've never met anyone like you."

"But you don't know me, Penny."

"How would I know you unless we slept together and made love. Much could be learned in my bedroom, I think."

"You're an unusual woman, Penny. You're very observant and you have a bold streak in you. I like that in a woman."

"Oh, I am not so bold. I'm very timid, in fact. But I think you would be tender and loving with me. Yes, that is what I have observed. You were that way with my father and . . ."

"I would like to sleep with you in your soft bed," he said. "I can't guarantee how much sleep we'll get."

She laughed and drank more of the bourbon. Her eyes took on a shine, and her face glowed with the rush of alcohol through her veins.

Slocum drank more of his drink and watched her to see if the liquor took her down or up.

Up, he decided, and that was a good sign.

"Another?" he asked.

"No, I've had quite enough of your good Kentucky bourbon. I'm tired and would like to go to bed now. Will you come with me?"

"No gentleman could refuse you, Penny," he said and finished his drink.

He stood up and walked over to her. He lifted her from the chair, and she was light and willing. He put his arms around her. She pressed into him, and he felt her soft breasts yield against his chest. She raised her head, and her eyes were moist, her mouth slightly open. He kissed her, and she squeezed him with her arms, pressed her lips hard against his.

He felt the heat of her seep through his clothes, warm his flesh. She was pliant and willing, he thought, as he held her fast and locked his lips on hers. Then, he felt her tongue dart into his mouth and lave his own tongue. So, he thought, she was experienced. At least in the art of kissing.

When they broke their kiss, she whispered to him.

"Come with me."

He followed her into a dimly lit bedroom with shades pulled closed over the windows. The lone lamp on the nightstand was turned low. It gave off a subtle scent of lavender flowers.

"Do you like the smell?" she asked.

"Very seductive."

"Good, because I want to seduce you."

He wondered how experienced she was. He wondered how many men she had lured into her boudoir.

As if reading his thoughts, she said, "You are the first man who has been in here. I'm afraid I have a strong fantasy life."

Slocum said nothing because she was unbuckling his gun belt with deft fingers. He reached down and helped her. He buckled the freed belt and she took it from him, hung it over one of the bedposts.

"You can take off your boots and clothes," she said as she turned down the bed. He sat down and pulled off his boots.

She sat on the edge of the bed and began to undress. She was all shadowy curves and angles as her arms and legs moved outside the small emblem of feeble yellow light. He shucked his clothes and left them in a dark puddle on the floor next to the chair.

He arose and walked to her, his cock throbbing and growing harder with each step. She took it in both her hands and kissed its crown. Her lips sent a shiver of electricity up his spine. His loins churned with desire.

She fell back on the bed and pulled him to her. They embraced and rolled to the center of the bed. She grasped his stalk and spread her legs, pulling him even closer.

"It's just as I had imagined," she breathed, and his cock throbbed with engorged blood.

"You have a pretty good imagination," he husked as he bent to kiss her.

"Ummm," she moaned. "The real thing is much better," she crooned as they kissed again.

Outside, the moon rose and cast a gauzy light into her bedroom. In the distance, a pack of coyotes yodeled, and it was sweet music to Slocum's ears. *The wild things are out tonight*, he thought, *and I'm among 'em.*

Penny was soft and yielding as he let his weight fall on her naked body.

5

They kissed long and with passion. She rolled beneath him and took him with her as she thrashed with desire.

"My panties," she breathed as she broke their kiss. "They're still on."

Slocum laughed and reached down. He felt the silky fabric, pulled her panties down past her knees, and then slipped them off her feet.

"Better?" he said.

"I feel like a fool," she said.

"You don't feel like a fool to me, Penny. You feel like a woman."

"Oh, I'm so hot, John. I've never been this hot."

"In a good way, I hope."

"A very good way," she said, and he felt between her legs, touched the wiry thatch of her pubic hair. He stroked the crease of her sex and she wriggled beneath him. She thrust her hips upward, and he slid his middle finger into her cunt. She was wet, and the wet was warm. He touched the tiny trigger inside, and she arched her back as a spasm of pleasure made her loins buck.

"Oooooh," she sighed. "You're touching it. The little man in the boat."

Slocum suppressed a laugh. He flicked his fingertip over the top of her clitoris and she shook all over. Warm liquid flowed over his finger as she gushed with precoital fluid.

"Oh, John," she screamed softly, "take me, take me."

"Not yet," he husked in her ear. "Not just yet."

"Oh, oh, oh," she exclaimed, her body writhing as if she were on a torture rack. Slocum stroked her clit, and her hips rose up and down. Her legs trembled with desire, the flesh of her inner thighs all a-quiver as if she were being electrocuted with a mild current.

"Oh, please, John, I want you inside me," she begged.

He took her through one last convulsion and then withdrew his finger. He pushed one of her legs aside, and she moved the other one. He mounted her and dipped his loins. She lifted her hips to meet him, and he sank his cock past the folds of her pussy. He slid inside slowly, and she clawed his back with her trimmed fingernails, raking his flesh until it was coursed with white lines.

"Yes, yes," she sighed, and let his weight fall on her body. He pumped into her with slow, steady strokes, and she screamed softly with each powerful thrust.

She was wet and warm, the satin lining of her sex smooth against the throbbing tumescence of his staff. He plumbed her depths, rising and falling in and out of her. She writhed and bucked beneath him, her sobs and sighs like the purr of a lioness. She gripped his hips and held him tight on the downstroke, then released him as he rose up again, only to plunge even deeper into the moist hot pudding of her sex.

He took it slow, forcing himself to hold back his seed. He was giving her pleasure and he wanted it to last. They fell into a rhythm of thrusting, yielding, their bodies melded into a single organism that rose and fell like the tide of the sea. She cried out when she spasmed with an orgasm, and he lost count of how many times she climaxed. Her body was sleek with sweat, and he rubbed her breasts with one hand, fondled her nipples until they were hard as acorns.

"Come, come," she said finally, and squeezed his buttocks with both hands.

He thrust his cock deep into her, stopped, then fucked her very fast until she was screaming with pleasure. He felt his seed boiling in its pouch, and as it rushed to its tiny mouth, he plumbed her to the core of her cunt. He ejaculated inside her as she climaxed once again.

For that single moment, he was floating somewhere high above the earth, a god-being without weight, his senses teeming with bursts of unearthly energy, his entire body given up to that one incredible moment when silent explosions rocked his being and his brain.

She lay beneath him, her eyes wide with wonder, her mouth open in a breathless final spasm that rippled through her like a jet of pure flame.

Slocum rolled off her body, his limp manhood spilling out of her sheath, wet and shrunken. He lay beside her on his back and felt the craving for a cheroot. He suppressed the urge to smoke and just lay there in a state of peaceful lassitude.

"It must have been your green eyes," she said, her voice soft in the moonlight.

"Huh?"

"Those green eyes of yours. They are so deep and mysterious, I just had to find out what you were like."

"And?"

"You are unlike any other man I've ever known. I would compare you to my pa and my uncle, but there's just no comparison. John, you have made me very happy."

"I'm glad," he said. "You're quite a woman, Penny."

"Thanks for that. I know you must have had many women and . . ."

He reached over and put a finger over her lips.

"Shh," he said. "This is about you and me, Penny. This moment, this time. This beautiful time."

She sighed.

"Ah, you make me feel so good inside. Thank you for saying that."

"It's what I feel. You're a beautiful woman and you've made me very happy."

"If you keep talking like that, I'll want you again," she said, a delicate gravel in her throat that made her words purr like a kitten.

"Give me time," he said. "I know I want you again."

"You don't want to sleep?"

"Not yet," he said.

His body was full of energy. He put a hand on her flat tummy and rubbed her there. She squirmed and made little sounds of pleasure that were not words, but animal noises that were beyond speech.

Her left hand floated to his loins. She grasped his lump of manhood and began to knead it with gentle rolls of her fingers.

Slocum felt his heart quicken. His blood seemed to turn hot. He reached over and fondled one of her breasts. The nipple hardened. He rubbed the tip of his finger over the rough nubbin.

"You're stirring up something again," she cooed.

"So are you," he said as blood surged into his penis again and it began to elongate and stiffen.

"Is this all it takes?" she said.

"Just a touch," he said. "Your touch."

"It's almost like magic," she said, and laughed.

Slocum said nothing. She rose up and leaned over him. She planted a kiss on his lips and massaged his cock, stroking its length up and down as if it were a piston in her hand.

He felt her grip tighten, and her hand began to move even faster until he was rock hard once again.

"Careful," he told her. "You may empty the vessel before you've had the chance to drink."

She stopped jacking him off and pulled on him to mount her. She tugged at his hip until he rolled on top of her. She spread her legs, opening her lower body like a morning flower. He sank to her and she guided him inside. He slipped into the yearning cavern of her sex, and she tightened her muscles and gripped him. He stroked in and out of her in slow, steady probes. Her loins rose to meet his, and they set up a special and private rhythm as if they were reclining dancers moving to the slow strains of a musical composition.

"John," she cooed. "It's so good. I never knew it could be this good."

They were both bathed in sweat, and the moonlight glistened on their naked bodies, imparting an unearthly glow that seemed to transport them into another dimension, a place where only they existed, a small and private place where the world outside had vanished, was invisible. She was soft, he was hard, and yet their twin passions blended like the night and the moonlight, two beings who had become a single glowing ember in a cluster of blazing suns.

He thought only of her during those moments. She was singular, yet she seemed to be an amalgam of all the women he had known, all the ones he had desired and conquered. He possessed her, but she possessed him, too. There was no time. No clocks chimed, no watches ticked. There was only the two of them on a timeless island in the midst of the universe, each moment precious, each one somehow eternal.

She squealed and cried out, then she screamed softly and groaned with each volcanic orgasm, a wildness in her that could not be tamed. He thrust deep into her and lingered as she convulsed in ecstasy, her pliant body quivering with the pleasure that shot through her, and when she reached a final pinnacle, his seed burst in its sac and spewed into her like warm honey, like the milk of mankind, and they shuddered together on that breathtaking summit, two souls that had become as gods, floating high above the world, part of the dark velvet of the night, illumined inside and out by billions of exploding stars.

They descended from the heights slowly, floating like feathery ashes from that magnificent bonfire of the senses where all reason was lost, and nothing mattered but that one exquisite moment, a moment so elusive it could never be caught or captured, lost to memory, lost to time itself.

They lay together in a peaceful lassitude and fell asleep, the perspiration drying on their skin as a warm breeze wafted through the window. He dreamed, and Penny was in the dream, and so was the blind horse and the river, the vast desert that bloomed with fiery flowers and pulsed with his own heartbeat like some ancient drum calling to him across the ages, and he was a child in Calhoun County, Georgia, before the war, and his mother was alive, and his father, his brother, and the woods grew into the desert and the tall pines grew out of solemn shadows and deer ran through the woods, their white tails flashing like lights bobbing on a lake.

He awoke before dawn, dressed, and strapped on his pistol. He tiptoed through the house and walked outside into the balmy predawn air, his nostrils full of the scent of sage and sand, of flower scents and the musty smell of horse droppings and his own dried sweat.

He lit a cheroot and pulled the smoke into his lungs.

He was full and he was empty.

He thought of Penny, asleep inside, her father lost to laudanum, the house so still and quiet, it loomed gray in the moonlight and seemed full of a peace that could not be measured.

He walked toward the back of the house, where Ferro whickered at him and tossed his head in greeting. He stood there, listening to the far-off yap of a coyote, and let the smoke wreathe him with its filmy strands, the smell of it intoxicating in that warm air that seemed to cloak him with an almost palpable energy. He felt alive and vibrant with some mysterious force that flooded his bones, his muscles, the sinew that held them altogether.

Then, he heard it, a soft crisp crackle that was a footstep. He tensed for just a split second and then he heard the metallic snick of a pistol hammer being cocked.

He started to turn to face the danger he felt behind him, when something hard rammed him in the small of his back.

A thousand thoughts coursed through his brain at that moment with blinding speed and none of them made any sense.

"Mister, you even twitch and I'll blow a hole in you big enough to drive a wagon through."

Slocum froze and waited for the hammer to drop, for the sound of the explosion that would blot out all his senses and plunge his mortal self into the final everlasting abyss of death.

6

Slocum felt his pistol sliding from its holster as the man behind him lifted it free of the leather sheath.

"Let's see them hands float skyward," the voice behind him said.

Slocum raised his hands with the cheroot still stuck in his mouth. The smoke tore at his eyes like shaven onions.

"I'm not a twitcher," Slocum said through half-clenched teeth.

"Turn around," the voice said. "Real slow-like."

Slocum turned around, his hands still held high. He felt the pressure of the gun barrel vanish from his back. Now, he stared at the man holding the pistol. In the dim light, he could see a grizzled face, most of it festooned in a long gray beard. The man's eyes were two black sockets.

"You must be Obadiah Swain," Slocum said.

There was a brief silence before the man said anything.

"You have the advantage, mister," the man said.

"I'm John Slocum."

"The name doesn't ring any bells. What in hell are you doing in my brother's house?"

"It's a long story," Slocum said.

"Well, you better give me some of it, because I don't know who the hell you are, or what you're doing here."

"Penny asked me to stay. She rescued Jethro from the Socorro Saloon. He was kidnapped, drugged."

"Jethro?"

"Yes. They tortured him. They wanted to know where they could find you."

"Bastards," Swain spat.

"Jethro's in bad shape. Lucky that his daughter's a nurse."

"How do you figure in this, Slocum?"

"I met Penny with your brother down by the Rio Grande. I brought them here. Penny asked me to stay."

"I been watching the house for some time," Swain said. "And listening."

Slocum said nothing.

Swain still had his pistol pointed at Slocum, and he had Slocum's Colt in his left hand.

"You deflowered my niece," Swain said, his voice flat and almost toneless.

"That would be the lady's secret, Swain."

"Except I know that you put the boots to her."

"Again, you might want to ask Penny about such a delicate matter."

"You talk like you might be a gentleman, sir."

"I wouldn't boast of such a label. I'm just a man," Slocum said.

"Well, I'll check your story. Meanwhile, I'll hold on to your pistol until I verify what you told me."

"That's all right with me."

"Just hold on there for a minute," Swain said. He turned his head and let out a low whistle.

Two men emerged from the shadows of the lean-to and walked toward him. They carried rifles and wore pistols.

They came up to Swain and stood there.

"Juan," Swain said, "you and Carlos guard the house. One in front, one in back."

The two men nodded in unison.

"Come on, Slocum, let's you and me go inside and see what's what. You first."

The two men walked single file to the front of the house, trailed by one of the Mexicans. Slocum went into the front room and stood in its center.

"Penny's probably still asleep," Slocum whispered.

"Light one of them lamps," Swain said.

Slocum's cheroot had gone out. He set the butt in an ashtray and lit one of the lamps on a table near the sofa.

"Where's Jethro? In that little room where Penny keeps all her medicants?"

"Yes," Slocum said.

"Let's look in on him. Walk easy, Slocum."

"She gave him laudanum, so he's probably still conked out," Slocum said.

Swain motioned for him to move, and Slocum walked down the hall to the sick room.

Penny stood next to her father's bed. A lamp glowed with a yellow light and cast her shadow on the wall.

"Uncle Obie," she said in a calm voice. "I'm glad you came. Pa's just barely awake. Put away that gun, will you?"

"I just ain't sure about Slocum here," Swain said. "I want to check out his story."

"Whatever John told you is true," she said. "He saved our lives."

"If you say so," Swain said. He holstered his pistol. Slocum stared at him, then dropped his eyes to his own pistol.

Swain handed it over, butt first, and Slocum slipped it back in his holster.

He looked into Swain's eyes. They were blue, like his brother's and his niece's. There were wrinkles at the edges, and Slocum saw the pink of his lips peeking from his full beard. He didn't resemble Jethro, but their faces both had a similar shape, and his dark hair was streaked and peppered with graying strands. His face, the portions that showed, was deeply tanned, as was his wattled neck and hands, his forearms. He was wearing loose clothing that was flaked with reddish and brown dust. He wore work boots that were scuffed and dusty, well worn.

Swain walked over to be closer to Jethro. He gazed down at his brother and took off his battered felt hat, which bore sweat stains around the brim.

He leaned over until his face was inches from Jethro's.

"Brother, can you hear me?" Swain said.

Jethro's eyelids fluttered like tiny wings. His eyes opened and Obadiah recoiled as if shocked at what he saw. Jethro's eyes were wet and red-veined as if they had been boiled and steamed. Shadows flickered in their pale blue depths and fixed on Obadiah's face in a locked stare.

"Obie?" The voice that came out of Jethro's clenched throat was raspy and seemed disembodied as if it had come from a different place.

"Yeah, Jethro, it's me," Swain said. He put a hand on his brother's, a gentle touch that was meant to comfort the injured man. "You feelin' better now?"

"Where am I? I—I don't remember much. Cigarettes burnin' me. All over."

Obadiah looked over at Penny, his eyebrows arched like the upper curves of question marks.

"They tortured Pa," she said.

Obadiah swore under his breath. He patted Jethro's hand and stood up.

"You're safe now, brother. You're home. Penny is takin' care of you."

Jethro closed his eyes. He seemed to drift off somewhere, his features a blank mass of discolored putty, gray and bluish, purple and brownish. His lips were cracked and there was a line of feverish sweat just above them.

"He needs rest more than anything," Penny said.

Penny and Obadiah walked from the room. Slocum followed them, the scent of alcohol and medicinal salve strong in his nostrils. The lamp burned on, leaking spiderwebs of smoke through its blackening chimney. He left the door open.

They sat down in the front room.

"You want some coffee, Uncle Obie?" Penny asked. "John?"

"I could use a taste," Swain said.

Slocum nodded as he studied Swain, who had placed his hat back on his head. He looked a hundred years old in the lamplight, but Slocum saw a wiry, energetic man who wasn't much older than Jethro. No more than a year or two, he figured. Swain leaned back in the overstuffed chair, one that he seemed used to, and stretched out his legs.

"What's that blind horse doin' out there in the stalls?" Swain asked.

"I'm supposed to kill it. I got him in Fort Craig. The liveryman didn't have the heart to shoot it."

"I saw the Army brand on its hip."

"That blind horse got us here."

"You going to shoot it?"

"I haven't decided," Slocum said. "That horse got us all here." He looked at Penny, who nodded in agreement.

"If John hadn't helped Pa and me, we'd probably both have been kidnapped or killed. We were followed here and John stood them off."

"What do you mean?" Obie asked.

Penny told him about Shadow and Roger Degnan.

"That's Roger's pistol over on that table," she said. "He dropped it when John shot him."

Swain walked over and picked up the converted Remington.

"That's Roger's pistol all right," he said. "That kid ain't right in the head. He's plugged a couple of people that I know of. Drunks who couldn't defend themselves. His brother Patrick ain't no better. Worse, maybe."

Swain set the pistol down and walked over to Slocum, looked down at him.

"Son, looks to me like you stirred up a hornet's nest. The Degnans, Patrick and Roger, are bad enough, but Morgan Sombra, good old Shadow, is one mean sonofabitch. And if you plugged Roger, it's for sure old Paddy Degnan will be on you like a streak of lightning."

"Roger made the first move," Slocum said. "If I hadn't shot him, I'd be six feet under by now."

Swain let out a sighing breath and sat down in his special chair.

He said nothing for a few minutes, then spoke to Penny.

"I brought you and Jethro some silver bars," he said. "They're out in my saddlebags."

"That's very kind of you, Uncle Obie."

He waved a hand in the air.

"That's no nevermind. I wonder if Jethro told that bunch at the saloon where I hang my hat."

"No, Uncle," she said. "Pa never told them where you lived."

"Good," Swain said, then turned his attention to Slocum.

"If we don't nip this in the bud, that crowd in Socorro won't give up. They'll come after you and me both. There's a big old snake in that saloon. And it's run by a bastard name of Wilbur Scroggs. He's the reason I took to smeltin' my own silver ore. That bastard robbed me once when I come back from Albuquerque with a mule load of silver."

"And he got away with it?" Slocum fished a cheroot from his pocket, but did not light it.

"I couldn't prove it, but I recognized Willie as one of the men who held me up. Shadow was the other one, and I suspect Paddy Degnan was the third man. I built my own smeltering plant, hired some Mexes, and made a small fort out of my adobe hutch. But they know that by now, and I expect their greed is gnawing at their guts again."

"Well," Slocum said as he bit off the end of the cheroot, "I sure wish you luck."

"Just like that, eh?" Swain said. "You ridin' out?"

"I was on my way to Albuquerque to look over some horseflesh up there."

"John, you can't leave now," Penny said, her face blanched to a bloodless frost.

"Why not? Might be better if I rode out today. If your uncle says I'm a target, that's one less thing you have to worry about."

Penny opened her mouth to say something, but Swain waved a hand to silence her.

"Yeah, Slocum, you can light a shuck, but if you think that's the end of it, you've got another think a-comin'. Roger Degnan is a loose cannon with the brains of a weasel. He's two pints short of a quart and will hunt you down wherever you go. And Sombra, he's a back shooter, a sneaky bushwhacker who'll mark your trail and lie in wait."

"So, what are you suggesting, Obadiah?" Slocum said.

"Call me Obie, Slocum."

"Call me John, Obie," Slocum said in a gesture of friendliness.

"I'm suggesting that you and I ride into Socorro and have a drink at that saloon and see what flies out of the hornet's nest."

Penny gasped.

"Take the fight to them?" Slocum said. "Two against four or five or more?"

"Might be our best shot," Swain said. "By now, Roger's bought himself another two-dollar pistol and he'll come gunning for you, sure as I'm sitting here."

"You're buying into my fight, seems like."

"Don't forget what those jaspers did to my brother. You weren't the main target, Slocum, but you sure as hell stepped into their sights by shootin' that little bastard Roger."

Slocum spat the tip of his cheroot into an ashtray and worked a box of matches out of his shirt pocket. He lit the end of the cigar and waved the flame out of the match and set it in the ashtray. He took a deep puff and looked straight at Obie, stared hard into his lamplit eyes.

"You have a point, Obie," Slocum said. "But to just walk into the lion's den and start the ball doesn't seem the right way to go about it."

"All right, what do you suggest, then?"

Obie's eyes were narrowed to feral points of light. His beard gave him an animal look, and Slocum decided he might well be a man to ride the river with. There was no yellow stripe down Obie's back.

"We can talk about it on the way to Socorro," Slocum said. "I'd like to take a look and see just what we're up against."

"John," Penny said, "you can't trust anybody in that saloon. They're all in cahoots. Even the women, the loose women, who work there. And there's one you have to look out for especially."

Obie nodded.

"Yep, she's right," Swain said. "Littlepage is one dangerous woman. She's as beautiful as all get-out, but I wouldn't trust her as far as I could throw that blind horse out in the shed."

"Who?" Slocum said.

"Linda Littlepage," Penny said. "She's a witch."

"Beautiful as all get-out," Obie said again.

Now that Slocum's curiosity was piqued to a high level, he knew he had to ride with Obie into Socorro and see Linda Littlepage for himself. And, too, he would see who came out of the woodwork at that notorious saloon where evil seemed to lurk.

7

Swain walked outside and whistled. Juan Gomez appeared a moment later.

"Bring in the silver, Juan," Swain said. He walked back inside.

"I'll fix us some breakfast," Penny said when her uncle came back inside. A few moments later, Juan knocked on the door. Swain let him in. He carried two bulging flower sacks.

"Set them on the dining table, Juan," Swain said.

The sacks made a thunk on the dining table when Juan plopped them down.

"Thank you, Uncle Obie," Penny said from the kitchen. "I'll put those in our safe."

"And hide the safe," Swain said.

"Oh, it's in a good safe place," she said, and then there was the clatter of pots and pans, the creak of cabinet doors.

"It is quiet," Juan said.

"That's when you must take a knife and sharpen your

eyes, Juan. I'll get you and Carlos some grub pretty soon."

"My stomach awaits your call, Obie," Juan said. He grinned as he walked back outside to take up his post.

"Good man," Swain said.

"You're pretty careful, Obie," Slocum said.

"If anybody's riding this way, from any direction, I want to know in plenty of time."

"White men don't like to fight in the dark," Slocum said. "And few of them come at you when the sun's just coming up."

"Out here, in the desert, you can never be sure," Swain said.

Slocum had been aware that Swain had been studying him while giving the impression that he wasn't staring a hole in him. Several times, he would look away from Swain, and when their eyes met, Swain would turn away with a suddenness that exposed his unusual interest.

There was a clatter down the hall and Slocum caught a glimpse of Penny carrying a bedpan out of her father's sick room. He heard kitchen noises as he smoked a cheroot and drank coffee with Swain. Penny had left them two cups and a pot on a woven rope pad so they could get their own refills without having to call on her. Slocum saw her bring back the bedpan, which gleamed dully in the dim light of the hallway. More noises came from the sickroom, along with the soft undertones of her hushed voice.

Then she called them to the breakfast table, and the two men carried their cups with them when they entered the small dining room and sat down opposite each other.

Silently Penny served them *huevos rancheros*, *tortillas*, *frijoles refritos*, and *salchiche*, pork sausages that were fat and hot to the taste with chopped-up hot chili peppers. She served herself and sat down to eat with them, a fresh pot of coffee in the center of the floridly tiled table.

"Penny," Swain said, "I'm going to leave the boys here to look after you and Jethro. Keep your guns loaded and don't let nobody in while we're gone."

"You're going into Socorro?" Penny said as she touched a fork to her food.

"This afternoon, yeah. How's that hotel comin'?"

"It's not finished," she said. "I think he's short of money. He's got adobe bricks stacked all over, but only one floor is finished."

Swain turned to Slocum as he chewed on a chunk of sausage.

"Willie Scroggs has big ideas. He wants to build a big hotel next to his saloon, with a connecting hallway and a dining room. Three stories."

"So, he needs more silver," Slocum said.

"That's hittin' the nail square on the head, Slocum. Willie's got the town in his pocket, but with no population to put profit in that pocket. He's a schemer, that one."

"And you think he's behind the kidnapping and torture of your brother?" Slocum said.

"No question about it. Anything illegal in Socorro, you can bet Scroggs is behind it. The man has no scruples, no conscience, and no loyalty to anything except money."

"He's a dangerous man," Penny said. "And he surrounds himself with gunslingers, like Shadow and the sheriff."

Slocum forked some eggs into his mouth. Penny sipped her coffee. She looked pale and wan in the morning light streaming through the window. Her hair shone like spun gold in a single ray of sunshine that streamed through the open window.

"Degnan's the big problem there. His deputies are on every wanted dodger from New Orleans to Bozeman," Swain said. "Gunslingers, yeah, and, like Shadow and Roger, back shooters, dry gulchers."

"Why do people stay in Socorro?" Slocum asked. "It doesn't sound like a nice town to live in."

Penny spoke up between bites of food.

"The town has mostly Mexicans in it, and they're scared of Scroggs and Degnan. The church is powerless. Scroggs pays good wages when he's flush with money, and that gives him power."

"The few men who have stood up to Scroggs are dead," Swain said. "He makes sure everybody who lives there knows it."

"What about the law?" Slocum asked. "Federal marshals? State troopers? The Army, for that matter?"

"The law requires proof, Slocum," Swain said. "And Scroggs covers his tracks like a fox."

"He gets away with murder," Penny said.

"Any questions, Slocum?" Swain asked.

Slocum looked at Penny.

"Yes. Where do you get eggs like these, and the pork?"

Penny laughed.

"Oh, you don't know, do you?" she said. "In back of Uncle Obie's stables, there's a garden and a henhouse that's fenced in with chicken wire."

"Jethro's got a good twenty acres," Swain said. "And a couple of springs, good irrigation. I have twice that much land and five times as much fresh water."

"I'm surprised," Slocum said.

"The desert is full of surprises," Penny said. "When you and Uncle Obie come back, I'll make some biscuits and maybe some bear claws."

"I can't wait," Slocum said.

As the two men were leaving the adobe house, Penny drew Slocum aside.

"Thank you for last night," she whispered in a conspiratorial tone of voice.

"Thank you, Penny," he said, and pecked her on the cheek with an avuncular kiss as fleeting as summer dew on cactus flowers. She squeezed his hand as the horses outside switched their tails and pawed the ground with impatience.

He and Swain left late that same afternoon. Slocum wondered what they were getting into since Obie wasn't exactly a font of information. But he knew the man had something on his mind because he kept looking at Slocum, stealing sidelong glances when he thought Slocum wasn't aware of his scrutiny.

"No use getting to town much before sunset," Obie said when they were clear of his brother's spread. "Town is dead until after sundown."

"I don't see much reason for there to be a town there at all," Slocum said.

"The Mexes take siestas during the heat of the day and don't do much work. Saloon caters to card players and drunks most of the day. At night, the ranchers come in to drink and take their pleasure with the whores. Ebb and flow, Slocum, ebb and flow. Like clockwork."

"Sounds like most folks around here have a pretty miserable existence."

"Them what don't have farms or ranches weave blankets and make pottery to sell in Albuquerque, Santa Fe, or Taos. They don't make much money, but they manage to stay alive."

Swain rode away from the road onto rough ground. His horse stepped around prickly pear, Spanish bayonets, and cholla.

"We don't want to ride the road," Swain said. "Too much of a target."

"A hell of a way to live, Obie."

"Yeah, but you live longer. I don't expect anybody's lookin' for us just yet, but you never know."

Slocum said nothing. They rode farther away from the road over a desolate landscape. The sun was sliding toward the horizon behind them, and their shadows stretched long and rumpled over the harsh ground. There was something about the way Obie rode that jogged a memory, a distant memory, in John's mind. Obie's back was straight and stiff. He held the reins loosely in his left hand and seemed part of his horse, a sorrel gelding that stood at least fifteen hands tall, with small feet. Slocum thought the horse must be part Arabian, perhaps part Morgan. A fine animal. Then, it struck him. Obie rode like a cavalry officer, and that brought back even more memories. Painful memories.

Swain looked at Slocum and then said something that made Slocum wonder if the man was reading his thoughts.

"I knew your older brother, John," Swain said. "Robert and I were in the same outfit at Gettysburg. I saw him go down. Couldn't help him."

"You rode with Pickett?"

"I did," Swain said. "Old George knew that Lee was wrong, orderin' us across that empty plain straight into the Yankee guns. It was brutal and senseless. Pickett knew it, but he charged up that hill anyway. Robert was brave and he talked about you a lot. He said you were a sharpshooter, made Captain."

"I found Robert on that battlefield," Slocum said. "He was already dead. He lay with a bunch of others cut down by grapeshot, like wheat cut with a scythe."

"Lee thought he would win that day. He truly did."

"Pickett knew better," Slocum said.

"George was pretty broken up afterwards. He didn't whine or whimper, but I could see the pain in his eyes. The man was grievin' real bad inside."

"So were we all," Slocum said.

"Your brother set great store by you, John."

"I still think about him a lot, and our pa, William, our ma, Opal. There are some empty places in the world where they were."

"True. I lost many friends in the war. And I still miss most of 'em."

The dark western horizon was a funeral bier blazing with the fire from the sun. A jackrabbit jumped from a clump of nopal and hopped in front of them, then froze against a rock, almost invisible in its shadow. In the distance, a quail piped and doves flew through the saguaros like gray darts, their gray wings whistling like tiny flutes, the notes fading as they twisted out of sight.

As they rode into the gathering dusk toward the town of Socorro, Slocum wondered whether Obie's talk of the distant War Between the States was not a warning to him of what might lie ahead, a veiled augur that they were riding to another war, a war where death could come with a single lead bullet from an impregnable fortress, not of rock walls and trees, but from drab adobe walls and incorporeal shadows.

Socorro was an unknown region to Slocum, a place of danger, where sharpshooting skills were useless and a man's back had a bull's-eye painted on it for every wily gunslinger to see.

It was dusk when they entered the town, the sounds of their horses' hooves thudding on dusty streets that crawled with vermicular shadows. The sonorous melodies of a guitar floated on the evening air in a minor key. A hush seemed to envelop the city until they turned down the main street toward the lamplit hulk of the Socorro Saloon, where riderless horses and mules stood at the hitch rails like mourners at a funeral.

8

Paddy Degnan strode into the hospital room. He carried a package under his arm. He walked to the farthest bed in the room, where a Mexican doctor stood next to Roger Degnan. The doctor, Alonzo Jimenez, was stooped over, his head close to the bandaged wound in Roger's side.

"No sign of blood poisoning," Jimenez said. "You are lucky. The bullet passed through the flesh and did not strike a vital organ."

Paddy heard the doctor's words as he stood at the foot of his brother's bed.

"It is good that you have a little fat around your middle," Jimenez said. "Or that you are the victim of a man who shoots poorly."

Jimenez, a young man in his mid-thirties, stood up and looked at Paddy.

"So, Roger can come home?" Paddy said.

"He wears stitches in his side. As long as he does not

become an acrobat for two or three weeks, his wound will heal very soon."

Roger flashed a weak grin at his brother. His face was pale, his blue eyes slightly bloodshot.

"Well, Roger, was the man who did this to you a poor shot?"

"He was a quick shot," Roger said. "He sure buffaloed the hell out of me." This last sentence was delivered in a wry tone as Roger remembered the incident. "I should have plugged him, but his hand was like lightning."

Both men had pale orange hair. Roger's hair was wiry, tousled, unruly. Paddy's was pasted down flat with pomade and covered by his Stetson. The two resembled each other, although Paddy's features were scarred and distorted by previous fistfights, while Roger's face was smooth and still bore the copper coinage of freckles, though these were faded and few.

"Roger," Jimenez said, "you can go home, but you walk very slow, do not ride a horse. You might pull those stitches loose. Keep the wound dry and the nurse will give you some salve to put on it once or twice a day."

"Thanks, Doc," Roger said. He looked at his brother. "Will you walk me home, Paddy?"

"I ought to kick your sorry ass home," Paddy said. "I got something to show you."

"I'll have the nurse ready for you when you leave," Jimenez said. He had been educated in the East and his Mexican accent was slight. He was from a privileged family in Mexico City. His mother took him to New York when he was small so that he could learn to speak English and improve his lot in life. But he had encountered prejudice and had come out West, where he could live among his own people and the whites and speak his native language. He wasn't bitter about his rejection at the Eastern hospitals but, under his mother's influence, was practical about it. He was content to practice medicine in this desolate place, which was still more prosperous than most of the small towns in Mexico.

"Is that young nurse, Penelope Swain, on duty?" Paddy asked.

"No, she has taken leave," the doctor said.

"Leave? You mean she quit?"

"I think only for a week or two. Why? Did you wish to see her?"

"No," Paddy said. "I just wondered."

"Well, I must go and put an order in for the medicine your brother must take home with him."

"See ya, Doc," Paddy said as Jimenez walked through the room, past beds with aging Mexicans and derelict white patients.

"Paddy, will you get my clothes out of that cabinet by my bed?" Roger asked.

"In a minute, boy. I got something for you."

Paddy walked around the bed to stand in front of his brother. Roger's scrawny legs dangled over the edge of the bed. He slipped into his white hospital gown to avoid shivering from the cold. He smelled of strong medication, and there was peach fuzz on his chin and jowls. His hair looked like an explosion of copper wire.

"What did you bring me?" Roger asked as he scooted forward an inch or two.

Paddy opened the sack and poured the contents onto Roger's pillow. Roger's eyes grew wide and flickered with a happy light.

"To replace that piece of junk you lost," Paddy said.

There, on the pillow, was a brand new Colt .45, the latest Peacemaker model, with stag grips, and a box of Winchester cartridges. The pistol gleamed a bright black in the lamplight. Roger picked it up with his right hand and looked at the fine even bluing of the barrel. He thumbed the hammer back to half-cock and spun the cylinder. The pistol gave out a reassuring purr.

"Boy, that's really something, Paddy. Is it mine?"

"All yours, boy. I cleaned it up for you, but it's a virgin. Never been fired."

"Brand new? Oh, Paddy."

"You can load it up later and we'll do some plinkin' when you're up to it. I got something else to show you before we leave this place."

"What's that?" Roger said as he eased the hammer back down. He rubbed his fingerprints from the barrel with the sleeve of his gown and set the pistol next to his bare leg.

Paddy reached into his shirt pocket and pulled out a folded piece of paper. He folded it back in half and showed Roger the drawing of a man's face. Above the drawing there was the legend WANTED—REWARD.

"Take a good look, Rog," Paddy said.

Roger studied the drawing of a man's face on the piece of paper.

"Yeah, that looks like the man who shot me. Only not as old. Who is he?"

Paddy took the paper and unfolded it.

"John Slocum," Roger said as he scanned the name beneath the crude portrait. "How did you know?"

"Sombra. He told me that he'd seen the man before and that there was a price on his head. Slocum's a wanted man. Killed a judge down in Georgia after the war."

"One thousand dollars," Roger said, as that was the legend at the bottom of the sheet of paper: REWARD—$1000.

"It may be a mite more by now. That dodger was in an old stack of them I found in a file cabinet. Left there by the previous sheriff."

Roger looked at the flyer again.

"Yeah, that's him. I'm sure of it," he said. "And with a bounty on his head. I'd sure like to get another shot at him."

"He's wanted alive," Paddy said. "Not dead."

"I'd still like to shoot him."

Paddy folded the paper and put it in his pocket. He patted the outside of his pocket.

"This gives me the right to throw down on that bastard and lock him up. I could use a thousand dollars about now."

"If I help, would we split it?"

"Sure, kid. We'd split it. Eighty/twenty."

"Eight hundred for you, two hundred for me?"

Paddy laughed.

He reached down and opened the cabinet. He pulled out Roger's bundle of clothes, his gun belt and holster.

"Here, get dressed, Roger, and I'll take you to home."

"I can't wait to put that pistol in my holster and feel its weight on my hip."

"Don't get in no big rush," Paddy said. "You got some healin' to do."

"Yeah. I'll heal real fast. Damn that John Slocum anyway."

"He shows up in Socorro and I'll clap him in irons," Paddy said as he watched his brother dress and strap on his gun belt. Just before they left, Roger slid the new Colt into its holster and grinned.

"It's a right good fit, all right, Paddy."

Paddy said nothing. He was wondering if he should put together a posse and go after John Slocum.

A thousand dollars would buy a passel of drinks at the Socorro Saloon.

9

Wilbur Scroggs slipped into his gold brocade vest and admired himself in the full-length mirror in his office on the second floor of the Socorro Saloon. The mirror was attached to one door of the wardrobe, and there were two such mirrors attached on the inside of both doors. Scroggs opened both doors and stepped between them. Now he could see his back reflected in one and his front in the other. He turned in a full circle.

"Still too fat," he decided.

"Just a little at the belt," a feminine voice replied. "That is a sign of success in Mexico."

Miranda Echeverria spoke from the sofa, where she reclined like some Mexican statue, her black stockinged legs stretched out, one cocked at an angle so that her short skirt slid down to her hips.

"The paunch?" Scroggs said. "It's a curse. I can't get rid of it. Spoils my profile."

"You look good, Willie," Miranda assured him.

She was a black-haired beauty, with dark sloe eyes and a flawless neck encircled by a red velvet choker. She had long black hair and the horse's tail was secured by two tortoiseshell barrettes, polished to a high amber sheen. She spoke with the accent of her native Jalisco, where she was born.

"That gut will go away once I put on my coat," Scroggs said, more to the mirror than to Miranda.

"You look very splendid, Willie," Miranda said. "*Muy guapo.*"

"Them Mex words sound like some kind of disease," he said in a humorless tone.

"They sound very pretty in Spanish."

There was a knock on the door. Scroggs slipped into his gray coat with velvet trim and continued to admire himself in the twin mirrors.

"See who it is, Miranda," he said.

She swung her legs off the sofa and walked to the door. A small balding man wearing a string tie and red garters on the sleeves of his white shirt stood at the door.

"The Chinaman's here," he said.

Miranda turned to Scroggs.

"Willie?"

"Send him up, Freddie," Scroggs said.

"Yes, sir," Freddie Wilcox said, and turned on his heel. Miranda left the door open and they both heard Freddie's footsteps thud in an uneven tempo on the carpeted stairs. A few minutes later, a small Chinese man trudged up the stairs with mouse-like furtiveness, his head turning to look down at the saloon floor, his eyes blinking as if they were afflicted with a nervous tic.

"Hello, missy," Wu Chen Fong said as he reached the door.

"Come in, Wu Chen," she said. She closed the door as

Wu Chen quick-stepped to the table. He was dressed in a tight black pin-striped suit that made him look like a diminutive banker.

"What have you got for me, Wu Chen?" Scroggs said as he stepped away from the mirrors and closed both of the wardrobe doors.

"Oh, very good opium, Mr. Scroggs," Wu Chen said. "Very good quality."

"Let's see it," Scroggs said.

Wu Chen opened the drab carpetbag and began pulling apothecary bottles from its innards. Strands of cotton trailed like smoke wisps from the bottles, indicators of the bedding in which he had placed them. He produced the bottles like a magician pulling objects from a top hat, his eyes animated in his acorn-shaped face with his small derby an almost comical allusion to that image. With delicate fingers, he arranged the bottles in a row like pawns on a chessboard, as if realizing that he was displaying secrets to human consciousness that could only be obtained by a selected few, for a price.

"Ah, you see," Wu Chen said as he passed a hand over the bottles, "I bring you the essence of the poppies that grew in China only few months ago."

"Is that all you brought, Wu Chen?" Scroggs asked, as if to deflate Wu Chen's confidence in his product.

"So many customers. Santa Fe. Taos. Albuquerque. Las Cruces. I save best for you, Mistah Scroggs."

Scroggs reached into his pocket. He withdrew a handful of bills bound together with a gold money clip. He slid the clip off as Wu Chen held out his hand, palm up, like some bellhop awaiting a tip. Scroggs placed one bill on Wu Chen's palm, then another, as Wu Chen's eyes danced like errant marbles in their sockets and his lips moved in a silent count.

"You want all bottles?" Wu Chen asked when Scroggs had stopped placing bills in his palm.

"Yes. All of those and more when you next come this way."

"Fifty dollah mo," Wu Chen said.

Scroggs counted out two more twenty-dollar bills and riffled through the folded wad for a ten. He placed that atop the other bills and Wu Chen closed his hand, grasping them as if they were birds' wings that might miraculously fly away. The bills disappeared into a pocket in his vest. He smiled and bowed in thanks, then closed up the carpetbag.

"Two months," he said as he left the room, opening the closed door with one hand, then whisking out of the room with short brisk steps. He made no sound as he descended the stairs, and Miranda watched him vanish amid patrons crowding the bar below.

"Can I have some, Willie?" Miranda asked as she glided back to the table, her stocking legs flashing in the twin slits of her skirt.

"No," Scroggs said, "I want you to work, not sleep. Besides, I can get my money back tenfold with this stuff."

"And use it to unlock secrets," she said, her eyes glittering like jewels as she looked longingly at the row of bottles filled with dusky powder.

"When necessary."

"But Swain got away," she said.

"He'll be back. He has a new master now." Scroggs pointed to the bottles.

"His daughter will break him of the habit. She's a nurse."

"I know. But opium is more powerful than a nurse. Swain will be back and I'll find out where his brother is mining all that silver."

She walked up to Scroggs and entwined her arm in his. She rubbed her leg against him.

"Maybe later, you will let me have some of that sugar," she purred.

"I'll let you have something, Miranda. Something better than that powder."

He swatted her on one buttock and she slipped away from him. He watched her walk to the door. He walked over and locked it when she was gone, then went back to the table. He twisted a dial left, then right, then left again, stopping on pertinent numbers, and opened a large safe and placed the bottles inside, next to other bottles, placing the new ones behind the old ones. He knew better than to eat any of the opium himself. He knew what the drug could do to a person.

He closed the safe and spun the dial, tested the handle to assure that it was locked. He went to the door, unlocked it, stepped outside, and locked the door with his key. He heard footsteps on the stairs and turned to see Morgan Sombra bounding up the stairs.

"Before you go down, Willie," Sombra said, "I got somethin' to tell you."

"Make it quick, Morg, I'm meeting someone."

"That hombre what shot Roger and helped Swain and his daughter get back home, he's got a price on his head."

"Oh?"

"Damned right. Degnan dug out an old dodger in his office, and sure as I'm breathin', that hombre's a wanted man. Murdered a judge down in Georgia."

"What's his name?" Scroggs asked.

"John Slocum."

"Degnan going after him?"

"He just got Roger out of the infirmary. I 'spect he'll whump up a posse and clap that rascal in irons come tomorrow."

"You'd better see that he does. And I want you to bring

Jethro Swain back here. I'll break that bastard if it's the last thing I do."

"What about his daughter, Penelope? She'll sure as hell try to stop me."

"Shoot her, Morg," Scroggs said. "Or bring her along with her pa. She might break quicker'n him."

"That's an idea. I wouldn't mind a taste of that myself."

"You keep your tongue in your mouth, Morgan. When I'm through with her, I don't care what you do to her."

"You got a deal, Willie," Sombra said.

"We'll see if I have a deal or not. Now step aside. I'm meeting somebody and I'm overdue."

Scroggs walked past Sombra and stepped down the stairs, holding on to the railing to keep himself grandly erect for his entrance. Sombra followed at a discreet distance.

"You little dictator," Sombra said under his breath.

He went to the bar and ordered a whiskey from one of the barkeeps, Eddie Tobin.

"Did you see where Scroggs went?" he asked as Eddie poured his drink.

"To his usual table. He's meetin' someone there."

"Yeah, I know. Who's he meetin'?"

"Feller named Hiram Littlepage."

"Linda's daddy?"

"He's Linda's uncle, I think."

"What in hell's her uncle doin' meetin' with Willie?" Sombra asked.

"I dunno. Mr. Scroggs doesn't exactly confide in me, Morg."

"Me neither. Hmm. Linda's uncle. Now, that's very interestin'."

"Everything's interestin', Morg. You just got to be interested in everything, that's all."

Eddie left with a smirk on his face. Sombra lifted his

glass and paused before he drank, mulling over what Eddie had said. He shook his head and splashed the walls of his mouth with whiskey.

One of the glitter gals, Maria Luisa Echeverria, sidled up to Sombra. She was Miranda's daughter and as pretty as any of the gals in the saloon.

"You drink by yourself, Morgan," she said. She held a small fan in her left hand. She opened and closed it in front of her face as her eyes peered over its pleated and painted expanse.

"Don't waste your time, Maria," he said. "There's plenty of pilgrims here tonight."

"But I like you, Morgan. You are much man."

"Flattery don't work none on me, gal."

"I do not flatter you, Morgan. I offer you my love and my heart."

"I got me a gal, Maria."

"A *gringa*," she spat. "She cannot give you what I can give you."

Morgan laughed.

"Okay," he said. "I'll invite you up sometime when I'm wrasslin' with her in my bed. I'll compare you both."

Maria laughed.

"Oh, you make the joke, Morgan."

"Your mother's comin' this way and she's got fire in her eyes. You better latch on to one of the payin' customers or she'll tan your hide."

Maria turned and saw her mother sliding through a clutch of men, each one eyeing her as she passed. Maria melted away from him and walked down the length of the bar, swaying and swishing her backside, fluttering her fan at every man who looked her way.

Sombra finished his drink and walked to the batwing doors at the saloon entrance. Men at the bar, the Mexicans, the drifters, the beggars, the thieves, all looked at him with furtive glances. He looked out at the tables. Most were empty at that early hour, but he saw Scroggs sitting at his table at the far corner, with a tall man he took to be Hiram Littlepage. The man sat straight, but he was a foot taller than Scroggs and he had the slick clothes of a gambler or a gunfighter, a wide-brimmed Stetson atop his head, and slender hands that looked as soft and graceful as a piano player's as they plied the air like twin birds performing aerial acrobatics.

There was no sign of Linda, but the other women in the saloon were looking at Littlepage with avaricious eyes, as if they wanted to bed him on one of the tables. The man was handsome, as handsome as Linda was beautiful, but his neatly trimmed sideburns and the starched cuffs of his white shirt tagged him as either a shrewd or a dangerous man. Or maybe both.

Sombra walked out of the saloon into the murky dusk. He headed toward Degnan's house. He knew the sheriff would be at home, probably with Roger, by now, and he wanted to see when he was going after that Slocum hombre and if there was any chance he might consider splitting the reward money with him.

As he walked along the street, some of the shops were still closing up for the night. A Mexican woman, whose husband owned a butcher shop, was throwing fish heads to a swarm of scrawny stray cats. When she had finished, she shook the basket over the cat's heads and he saw the glitter of fish scales falling like snow crystals onto the darkening street.

10

Slocum saw the shadowy figure of a man leaving the saloon. As they rode closer, past shops closing up for the day, he saw the man disappear in the shadows. Horses and mules stood at the hitch rails in front of the three-storied adobe that was the Socorro Saloon, switching their tails, standing hipshot, tossing their heads. One or two of them whickered as the two men rode to an empty stretch of rail.

"That man that just left the saloon," Slocum said, "did you see him?"

"I saw him," Swain said.

"I don't know, but I think that might have been—"

"It was," Swain interrupted. "That was Morgan Sombra."

"You know him?"

"I've seen him a few times. He don't say much, but he's always someplace you don't expect him."

"Well, he works for the saloon owner, doesn't he?"

Swain swung down from the saddle, his left hand gripping the saddle horn until both feet touched ground.

"Some say he works for Scroggs, but to me he's just another no-account drifter, a saddle bum with a six-shooter."

"He made no move against me yesterday." Slocum touched down and walked around to face Swain. "He just sat his horse until I shot the kid, then turned away with the kid in tow and headed back to town."

"Well, you had your pistol out, Slocum, and Sombra was facing you. That's not Sombra's way. They don't call him Shadow just 'cause that's his Mex name. That's where he lives. In shadow, where he can get a good look at your back and you can't see him."

"I'll keep that in mind," Slocum said as the two mounted the boardwalk and headed for the batwing doors and the buzz of conversation floating on the smoke and yellow lights from the saloon lamps inside.

On the opposite side of the street, a paneled wagon was parked. Two horses were hitched to it. On the side panel, the legend ORIENTAL PLEASURES was painted in large cursive lettering. Below that, these words were spaced evenly in a rainbow arc: *Incense, Exotic Teas, Elixirs, and Perfumes*. At the very bottom there appeared the name Wu Chen Fong, braced on either side by Chinese characters. Slocum glanced at the wagon and saw a man on the seat, smoking a cigarette. The glow left orange traces as it moved from hand to lips. Slocum said nothing, but the wagon prickled his curiosity and he filed the memory of it away in his mind.

Just before they reached the entrance to the saloon, Swain stopped. He put a hand on Slocum's elbow to stop him.

"Before we go in there, Slocum, there's something you ought to know."

"What?"

"Scroggs has two gunmen inside. There are three of

them that I know of, but there are always two on duty at one time. One is a tall rawboned Swede named Olaf Thorson. Blond hair, wide shoulders, slim waist, tied-down holster. Another is a thick-necked German named Gustav Adler. They call him 'Gus.' And the third one that I know of is a short, wiry, skinny man who goes by the name of Ruben Loomis. The bartenders, whose names I don't know, although I think one of them is named Cal—anyway, they always have a sawed-off Greener and a club within reach. I've seen them clear the room when the patrons got rowdy."

"Sounds like a saloon I visited in Dodge City," Slocum said.

"The Mexicans got Injun blood in them and don't hold their likker too good sometimes. They've carted a few of them out of there feet first."

"I'll keep my eyes peeled," Slocum said.

The two men entered the saloon, stepped to one side as they waited for their eyes to adjust to the light from the lamps.

"Let's head for the bar," Swain said. "I'll buy you a drink."

"Obliged," Slocum said and followed Swain as he walked to an empty space at the long bar.

One of the bartenders came up and wiped the bar top with a dirty towel. He looked at Slocum, then at Swain.

"Swain, isn't it?" the barkeep said. "I don't recollect seein' your friend in here."

"Cal, is it?"

"Yeah. Cal Meecham, Mr. Swain. Ain't you Jethro's brother?"

"How do you know my brother?"

"Oh, I seen him in here a few times. Ain't seen him lately, though."

"You're a goddamned liar, Meecham," Swain said, his

voice pitched low so that it didn't carry beyond the three of them.

Cal reared back as if he had been struck. Then he looked toward the end of the L the bar made. Slocum swung his head to track Cal's line of sight. In the dark corner at the end of the L, he saw a short wiry man who was smoking a cigarette.

"You call Ruben over here, Cal, I'll drop you where you stand."

Slocum readied himself to draw his pistol if the dispute went any further.

"What's your pleasure, gents," Cal said, a slight quaver in his voice. He was a short burly man with a beer belly and a small square moustache that looked as if he had a mouse in his mouth. His hair was thinning on top, and his sideburns were patchy as if they had fed a colony of moths.

"Old Taylor for me," Swain said.

"You got any Kentucky bourbon?" Slocum asked.

"We got bourbon," Cal said. "I don't know where it was born."

"Bring whiskey and bourbon then." Swain plunked a five-dollar gold piece on the counter. Cal's eyes widened. He turned and left to fetch the bottles. Swain turned around, his back to the bar. Slocum did the same.

"You see him over there in the corner?" Swain asked in a low voice. "Loomis?"

"I saw him," Slocum said.

Swain scanned the room. He stopped when he saw Scroggs and another man at Scroggs's usual table in the far corner of the room.

"That's Scroggs over yonder," Swain said. "That back table. He's the pudgy one with the gold vest. Don't know who he's with."

"I see him. He's the owner, eh?"

"Yeah."

Cal set glasses on the bar top and poured drinks.

"Bourbon's from Tennessee," he said. He grabbed up the gold piece and went to the cash register. He plunked the change, in silver, down on the counter.

"Leave the bottles," Swain said.

Cal slunk to the center of the bar and looked the other way. Slocum followed his line of sight clear to the end of the bar. There, he saw a tall blond man who looked Swedish. The man stood with his muscular arms folded across his chest as if he was looking for trouble to break out at any moment.

"That's Thorson down there," Swain said. "He's hoping for the chance to break a couple of heads."

"His muscles have got muscles," Slocum said.

Swain laughed.

"He used to wrestle for a livin'," Swain said. "Story is he killed a man in the ring."

"I wouldn't want him to give me a bear hug," Slocum said.

"Let's saunter over and have a word with Willie Scroggs."

"You looking for trouble, Obie?"

"If there's goin' to be a ball, might as well open it."

Slocum followed Swain across the sawdust-strewn floor, past empty tables. One or two Mexican drinkers looked at them, and a glitter gal or two flounced past in front of them, their eyes outlined with kohl, their lips plump and red as ripe cherries, their cheeks smeared with rouge.

Scroggs looked up when Swain approached.

Littlepage turned his head, looked at Slocum.

"I hear you been lookin' for me, Willie," Swain said. He stood so that he could see both Thorson and Loomis with a slight turn of his head. Slocum stood with his back to the wall, so that he could see if either man left the bar and made a move toward them. He looked at Scroggs, then at Littlepage. The latter's face was a blank. Scroggs looked slightly apoplectic.

"Why no, Mr. Swain," Scroggs said. "I ain't paid you no mind whatsoever. What brings you to town?"

"Dynamite," Swain said, much to Slocum's surprise. Obie hadn't mentioned it to him.

"Well, you won't find none of it here," Scroggs said. He looked at Slocum.

"I don't believe I've had the pleasure of meetin' your friend here."

"His name is Slocum and it would not be a pleasure for him to meet you, Willie."

Scroggs drew back in his chair, stung by the frank insult.

"Name's familiar," Scroggs said. "Face, too. I think I've seen it on a wanted poster."

Slocum said nothing. He watched the two men at either end of the bar, Thorson and Loomis. They still stood there, like cigar store Indians, stolid, blank-faced, but somehow threatening.

"John Slocum?" Littlepage asked.

Slocum did not reply or acknowledge Littlepage's presence at the table. He continued to watch the two gunmen, as if he were outside the hostile sphere of the table where Scroggs and Littlepage sat.

"I heard tell of a John Slocum when I was in Silverado," Littlepage said. "You were pretty handy with a gun, as I recall."

Slocum stood impassive, as if unwilling to acknowledge Littlepage's pointed remarks.

Scroggs looked up at Swain.

"You might be keepin' bad company, Obadiah," Scroggs said. "People are known by the company they keep."

"Scroggs, I'm just giving you fair warning. Leave my brother and his daughter alone. And as far as finding out where I live, I'll kill any of your men who come within range of my gun sights."

"Are you threatening me, Swain?"

Slocum turned and fixed Scroggs with a stabbing stare.

"If he isn't, Scroggs, I am," Slocum said. "I saw what you did to Jethro Swain. To me, you're nothing but scum, something I'd scrape off my boot in a cow pasture."

"Slocum," Scroggs said, "I want you and Swain to leave my establishment. If you don't, I'll have you thrown out."

"Fuck you, Scroggs," Swain said, and started walking back toward the bar.

Slocum waited another second before he followed Swain.

"I look forward to seeing you again, Scroggs," Slocum said. "If there's anything I hate, it's a man who tortures another the way you tortured Jethro Swain."

Scroggs glared at Slocum.

But Slocum turned his back on the two men and followed Swain to the bar.

A tall, voluptuous woman entered the saloon through the back door and made her way toward Scroggs's table. She had raven black hair with a red carnation affixed to one side. She wore a slinky silk dress that clung to her curves like a second skin of bright blue. She carried a small beaded purse and wore a pearl choker that emphasized her delicate neck and shone like stars above her bosom.

She walked straight up to Slocum, her gaze sweeping up and down him like a searchlight.

"My," she said, "you make the saloon look like a gathering place for midgets. I like a tall man and I see you know my uncle."

"No, I don't believe I know your uncle," Slocum said. "Or you."

She smiled at him and touched a pair of fingertips to her chest.

"Why, I'm Linda Littlepage, and I saw you at my uncle's table."

"I was there," Slocum said, "and if you had been there, I'd probably still be there."

"And who are you?" she asked.

"The name is Slocum. John Slocum."

She stiffened then, as if he had slapped her face with a wet towel, and her expression turned dour.

"It seems I've made a mistake," she said.

Slocum doffed his hat and took a step toward the bar, where Swain waited for him.

"Not yet," he said, and winked at her.

11

Swain wore just the trace of a smirk on his face when Slocum joined him at the bar.

"Obie," Slocum said, "don't say it. Just pour us another drink of that Tennessee likker."

"Oh, I wasn't goin' to say nothin' in particular."

"Like hell you weren't."

"I just saw you bump into the Queen Bee of the Socorro Saloon, that's all. She was shuckin' your duds with her eyes for fair."

"She's the boss lady here?"

"She runs the glitter gals. I reckon that's her uncle she's jawin' with right now."

Swain poured fresh drinks in their glasses and laid a ten-dollar bill on the bar top.

Slocum saw Linda talking to Scroggs and Littlepage. Every few seconds she glanced in his direction.

"I wonder if she knows what her uncle does for a living," Slocum said.

"Do you know?"

"When I was in Silverado, he was running an opium den. We didn't cross paths, but I saw men come out of a shady saloon there like sleepwalkers. Someone told me they were smoking opium. The way I heard it, they were puffing the drug through a tube stuck in a water-filled fishbowl of some kind."

"That's the Chinese way, I hear. Didn't know there was opium dens 'cept in New York and Frisco."

"Well, there was one in Silverado, and it wasn't a Chinese place."

"Hmm. Interesting," Swain said. "Well, there's your drink, Slocum. Then we'd better light a shuck. Loomis and Thorson look like two hungry dogs a-watchin' us."

Slocum lifted his drink and glanced at the gunmen standing at both ends of the bar. And they were glancing in his direction, as well. He upended the glass just as Hiram Littlepage arose from Scroggs's table and walked toward the door. Linda stayed with Scroggs and sat down in her uncle's chair.

Littlepage walked through the batwing doors and Slocum forgot about him.

He was just finishing his drink when the batwings swung open and two men entered, Littlepage and a small Chinese man wearing a derby hat.

"Who's that with Littlepage, Swain?" asked Slocum.

"Damned if I know. Some Chink."

Littlepage and Wu Chen walked to Scroggs's table. Linda rose from her chair and left without a word to either her uncle or the Chinese man. She headed straight for where Slocum and Swain were standing, ignoring the other male patrons, who slid their glances over her like so many groping hands.

She wore a stern expression on her face that turned it

rigid, as if it had been waxed. There was a paleness beneath her rouge, and her teeth were scaling off some of the lipstick on her lower lip.

She stopped just in front of Slocum and looked up at him.

"Well, you met Hiram," she said. "What do you think of my uncle?"

"Frankly, Miss Littlepage, not much."

"It seems he has a low opinion of you, too, Mr. Slocum."

"Many people do," he said.

"Do you know what that man does for a living? How he makes his money?"

"Not for sure. I heard talk about him in Silverado a while back."

"He preys on people. Poor people, mostly. He ruins their lives and rakes in the money."

"I've heard that, too, ma'am."

She stepped closer, and some of the color began to return to her recently frozen face. A strip of lipstick dangled from her lower lip. She plucked it off and winced slightly as the loose skin separated from its moorings.

"Call me Linda, please. I'd like to get to know you better."

"Why, Linda?"

"Because Hiram doesn't like you and neither does Willie Scroggs."

"You work for Scroggs, don't you?"

"Actually, no. I don't work for Willie. The girls you see in here work for me and I hire them out to this and other establishments in town."

"I don't get it," Slocum said.

"My girls pay me a percentage of their earnings. They are paid more than the usual fees for their services. I negotiate their wages and they pay me for higher earnings."

"Then, you're a kind of madam, I take it," Swain said.

Linda's face took on a roseate hue as she wheeled on Swain.

"That's an insult, Mr. Swain," she said. "What the girls do in their spare time is their business. I don't ask, and they don't tell. Some of them are married, with little children. They're here to entertain and be pleasant to the patrons, that's all."

"That's all?" Swain said.

"The men who come here are lonely. Most of them don't have much money. They seek diversion and a kind word or two. Other girls who work for me are hairdressers and manicurists, secretaries and clerks. Women are not paid as much as men. I can't help that, but I can get them decent wages and decent treatment on their jobs."

"I think I get it now," Slocum said.

She turned to him and smiled.

He smiled back.

Then, she put a hand on his arm.

"I knew you had some decency in you, Mr. Slocum. And some understanding."

"My friends call me John," he said.

"John. A nice name. I don't like Jack or Johnny. Too many rough men are called by those nicknames."

"It's just John. It's always been John."

"Are you planning to stay here long?" she asked.

Slocum looked at Swain, his eyebrows arched like a pair of question marks.

"John, I've got some business to take care of tonight," Swain said. "I'll put us up in separate rooms at a lodging house in town, Casa Rosa, on Second Street."

"That's a nice place," Linda said. "Much nicer than any of the three small hotels here."

"So, you and Miss . . . er, ah, Linda, have your talk."

"I was going to invite you both to supper," Linda said. "Believe it or not, there's a cozy and nice French restaurant on Palo Verde here. The French couple who owns it are very nice, and two of my girls work there. Will you take supper with me, John?"

"Sure," he said. "It would be a pleasure, Linda."

"This was our last drink anyway," Swain said. He downed his drink and his eyes didn't water.

John lifted his glass.

He looked over the rim at the back table. He saw Scroggs lift his hand and make a sign that looked like a man pulling the trigger of a pistol. He tracked Scrogg's line of sight and saw that he was gesturing toward the Swede, Thorson.

Swain said, "Uh-oh," and turned toward Loomis. Swain stepped away from the bar.

"What is it?" Linda said as Slocum grabbed her and swung her behind him.

"I think Scroggs just told Thorson to gun us down," he said.

Thorson dropped his arms and stepped into full view at the end of the bar. He looked straight at Slocum.

Swain drew his pistol and held it high. He aimed at Loomis, who still stood there at the L, in shadow.

"You make one move, Loomis," Swain thundered, "and I'll put one right between your eyes."

A glitter gal screamed.

Miranda looked at Swain and yelled, "He's got his gun out."

Men dove under tables and the glitter gals all screamed like schoolgirls and raced for cover.

"Duck," Slocum told Linda, and pushed down on the top of her head.

Linda went into a squat as Thorson strode toward Slocum.

"You in the black," Thorson said. "I'm callin' you out."

Slocum took a step away from Linda and Swain. He squared off to meet the threat. Men fled the bar like quail taking flight until there was only empty space between the Swede and Slocum.

Cal, the bartender, bent over behind the bar. Slocum caught the movement out of the corner of his eye.

"You touch that Greener," Slocum said, "and you'll wind up six feet under sand and cactus."

Cal froze and didn't complete his move.

The Swede came on, step by slow step, his arms out to his sides like wings, his right hand cupped to draw his pistol.

"You heard me, mister," Thorson said. "You got two seconds to shit or get off the pot."

"One, two," Slocum said, counting off the seconds.

Thorson went into a fighting crouch and clawed for his holstered pistol.

"Three," Slocum said, and his right hand flew like a thunderbolt to his pistol. His hand was a blur and time seemed to stop in that split second. There was a hush in the saloon that hypnotized all who were present, buried them as if they were suspended in a deep black ocean of silence.

Swain cocked the hammer of his pistol, and the sound was like a steel door opening on eternity.

Loomis stared into infinity and did not move or twitch.

Linda sucked in a breath and trembled inside as if she were falling earthward from a high steep cliff.

Life hung in the room like a tiptoe on the edge of an abyss.

Slocum's eyes narrowed to dark slits as his fingers closed around the grip of his Colt.

There was no time to think.

There was no time to stop what was going to happen.

There was only death, and it crouched in that frozen split second of time like a slavering animal over its certain prey.

12

Slocum heard the soft whisper of his pistol as it cleared leather. He thumbed back the hammer of his Colt as his arm floated the pistol upward to waist-high.

Thorson's eyes widened as he drew his pistol, and for the briefest instant, his blue eyes clouded over as he heard the hammer click on Slocum's gun.

Slocum tilted his pistol and squeezed off a shot. The Colt bucked in his hand with its powerful recoil. But the bullet sizzled through the air on a true course and stuck Thorson right between his eyes. There was the smack of the bullet as it plowed into his forehead, leaving a neat black hole. It furrowed through his brain and turned it to mush before blasting out of the back of his head, spraying a mist of blood and brain fluids, along with shards of skull, like shattered pottery.

His hand went slack and his pistol fell from his grasp and clattered on the floor like a chunk of useless iron. Thorson's eyes widened and rolled back in their sockets. He collapsed in a heap, landing like a rag doll on the floor, all of his muscles limp, his massive body a heap of lifeless sinew, bone, and flesh.

Blood spurted from Thorson's nose and leaked from one of his ears. The smoke from Slocum's pistol hung in the air like a breeze-whipped spiderweb, then evaporated. Slocum spun around, pistol in hand, and aimed at first one bartender, then the other. Finally, he walked over to Swain and pointed his pistol at Loomis.

"Better light a shuck, Loomis," Slocum said. "Thorson's dead and you're next if you even twitch."

Loomis went pale in his face and shuffled away from the bar. His backside disappeared through the batwing doors, which swung for a few seconds then slowly came to a stop.

Linda stood up. Her hands shook and she fought to keep her knees from knocking together. She glanced at the dead man and then gazed at the table where her uncle and Scroggs were rubbernecking like a couple of parade gawkers. Wu Chen was nowhere in sight. The smell of burnt powder was strong in her nostrils, and she rubbed her nose between thumb and forefinger.

"Lordy," she gasped. "I never saw anything so fast, John Slocum. Thorson had the drop on you. I saw it clear as day. But you shot first and you hit him right between the eyes."

"This saloon has turned into a dangerous place," he said. "Obie, what say we take a walk outside."

Swain eased the hammer back down on his pistol and shoved it back in its holster.

"Yeah, I've had enough excitement for one night. You'll have a hotel room waitin' for you after you've finished your supper."

He looked over at Linda, who was clinging to Slocum's arm.

"Or whenever you're good and ready, that is."

Linda smiled wanly at Swain.

"Yes," she said, "let's have some supper. I'm shaking inside like a leaf."

The men under the tables still cowered there. All of them seemed to be looking at Slocum's pistol, which was still in his hand.

He looked over at the two bartenders.

"When we walk out of here," he said, "I'd better not hear those shotguns cocking."

"No, sir," Cal said, and the bartender nodded several times as if trying to make his head fall off.

"Let's go," Slocum said.

He and Linda followed Swain out of the saloon and into the inky cloak of night. There were no streetlamps. The three of them walked to the end of the block, then turned right down an even darker street.

"Follow me," Linda said after Swain had left their company. They could see the dim buttery light of the hotel midway in the block where Swain was headed.

She let Slocum take her arm and they walked in silence to a street where adobe buildings snugged up against each other. In one, lamplight shone through and cast a yellowish orange glow on the dirt street outside.

"There it is," she said, and pointed to the small restaurant near the end of the block.

The sign outside read: *Chez Soleil*.

"What's that mean?" Slocum asked.

"Sunny Place," she said.

"Good name, but it could have been named Starry Place, too."

He looked up at the billions of stars, the winding sheet of the vaporous Milky Way. In the clear desert air, the stars seemed closer, or larger. A balmy breeze wafted their way. It tousled Linda's hair, and she brushed strands out of her eyes.

There were tables on a patio outside, and each of them was covered with a large cinnamon-colored parasol.

"Shall we sit outside?" she asked.

"That would be nice, I think."

"I can ask Pierre to close the umbrella so that we can see the starry sky."

"That, too, would be nice," he said.

"You're more comfortable outside, in the open air, aren't you, John?"

"I suppose so," he said, trying to make his language more sophisticated since he suspected that Linda was an educated woman.

They sat down at a table near the cast-iron railing and soon a man appeared with a lamp and a slate. He wore a dark blue apron and his boots were shiny, his pants creased and pressed, his white shirt starched to a dignified crispness.

"I am André," the waiter said, his French accent very Parisian, to Slocum's mind.

"André, would you tell Pierre and his lovely wife, Giselle, that Miss Littlepage is here. And we'd like you to collapse the umbrella."

"But, of course, mademoiselle," André said. He quickly adjusted the struts of the parasol and collapsed its wings. Linda smiled at him as he handed Slocum the slate.

"Thank you," Linda said.

"We have the beef cooked in sherry wine," André said, "with *pommes frites*, the fried potatoes, and buttered peas. You would like a fine wine with your meal, *non*?"

"Yes," Linda said with a quick glance at Slocum, "if the gentleman agrees, a burgundy or a claret."

"Burgundy," Slocum said. "I do have some acquaintance with wines."

Linda laughed softly.

"Bring us the burgundy, André, *s'il vous plaît*."

"*Oui, oui,*" André said, and glided off the patio and into the restaurant. A few moments later, Pierre Lachaise, the owner of the café, appeared at their table.

"*Bon soir,* Linda," he said in the warmest of tones and with a toothy smile. "Giselle is preparing the meals tonight since my cook, Auguste, is indisposed."

"Oh, is he ill?" Linda asked.

"He is drunk, *ma'amselle,*" he said without missing a beat. "He cooks with the wine and he gulps it like a fish."

Slocum and Linda laughed, along with Pierre.

"I hope you enjoy your meal, Linda and the gentleman."

"Pierre, this is John Slocum, a new friend of mine."

"Do not get up, *M'sieu* Slocum," Pierre said. "I am happy to make your acquaintance." His accent was less pronounced than André's, but it was there, like fine oil on the small gears of a good watch.

"How did you wind up in Socorro?" Slocum asked.

"Ah, it was the fate, I think. We drive the wagon from Saint Louis and the dream was Oregon, *non*? So, the wagon, she break down here and we see how cheap to live and we buy the adobe and open the café. We see our countrymen pass through and they eat the food and we become very happy in this quiet place."

"Your place is an oasis in this desert," Linda said.

Pierre smiled. "*Merci, ma'amselle,*" he said. "You are very kind."

When the small talk was finished, Pierre walked back inside. The waiter served the food and wine while Slocum and Linda gazed at each other between bites and sips.

"You asked Pierre how he and Giselle wound up in Socorro," she said. "I'd like to know how it is that you are here at such a propitious time."

"Propitious time?"

"Scroggs is up to no good. He's a mean tyrant and I

know that he kidnapped that poor man, Jethro Swain, and fed him opium. He wants to find Obadiah's silver mine and hog it all for himself."

"Jethro is why I'm here," Slocum said, and told her the story of finding Penelope in need of help with her father.

"I like Penny. She seems a decent woman, and Jethro never harmed a soul here. But I was powerless to help him."

"Maybe it was fate that brought me here, like Pierre said."

"Do you believe in fate?" she asked.

Slocum shrugged. "I believe there are hidden reasons behind every turn in the road on the journey through life. It's not something I mull over too much, but when I look back, it seems there might have been unknown forces at work in my life."

"I feel the same way," she said. "I keep thinking that I have some purpose in life and that's why, when I saw the way women were treated out here in the West, I decided to do something about it."

"And it seems to be working?"

"Slowly," she said. "Very slowly. But I care about my girls and their lot in life. I call them girls, but of course, they are grown women. They just don't know how to stand up for themselves."

Slocum reached in his pocket for a cheroot.

"Mind if I smoke?" he said.

"I'd like to try one of those," she said. "I'll order us some brandy and we can let our meal digest."

"The cheroot might be too strong for you," he said. But he fished another cigar from his pocket and handed it to her.

"I'll risk it," she said.

"Bite off the end and put the tip in the ashtray," he said. "It will draw better."

The waiter appeared as Slocum lit her cheroot.

"Bring us some cognac, will you?" she asked him as he began to clear their plates from the table and set them on a large pewter tray.

"But of course," André said.

Linda choked on the smoke from the cheroot. Her eyes watered with tears and she gasped for a clean breath.

"My, it is a bit strong," she said as she fanned the smoke away from her face.

"Don't pull the smoke into your lungs," he said. "Just let it warm your mouth and then blow it out."

She puffed on the cigar and then spewed a small cloud of smoke out. Some of it went up her nose and she made a face.

"Better?" he said.

"Much better, John."

They sipped the cognac and smoked. Linda even inhaled some of the smoke and managed not to choke or cough.

"You're getting the hang of it," Slocum said.

"I'll walk you to your rooming house," she said as they finished their cognacs.

"Then you would have to walk home alone," he said. "In the dark."

"I'm not afraid, John. But I'm hoping you'll invite me into your room."

A few patrons came and went inside the café. There was the clatter of dishes and silverware. Bats knifed the night sky, scooping up flying insects, their leathery wings beating the air in quiet whispers.

"You'd still have to walk home alone," he said, testing the waters of her desire.

"Perhaps you will walk me home in the daylight," she said, and her invitational tone was a silken purr, laden with promise.

"Gladly," he said, and smiled.

She signed the check that André presented. "I didn't bring my purse," she explained. "I will pay Pierre the next time I come in."

"Thank you for supper," Slocum said.

"It was my distinct pleasure, John."

As they left the café, Slocum saw a shadowy figure across the street. A man flitted from one adobe building to another. Both Slocum and Linda saw the crouching, scuttling man. She stopped up short and Slocum's right hand floated downward to hover just above the butt of his pistol.

"That's strange," Linda said. "We'd better be careful."

"Get behind me," he said. "Whoever that is, he's up to no good."

"I know who it is," she said as she moved behind Slocum.

"Who?" he whispered.

"Loomis," she said. "Scroggs must have told him to follow us."

"Why?" Slocum asked, but he knew why.

"You killed Thorson, and Scroggs wants you to pay."

Slocum stepped into the shadows of another adobe, a closed shop that sold pottery and Indian blankets. He pressed Linda against the wall and drew his pistol.

"It's not me Loomis is after," she whispered.

"Wait here," he said. "I'm going after him. Maybe I can draw him out in the open."

"John, he'll kill you. Loomis is a dead shot and he won't come out in the open to murder you."

"Let's just see how bad the cat wants the mouse," he said, and stepped into the center of the street. He began to walk where he had last seen Loomis. He held his pistol straight down at his side, his finger inside the trigger guard. He eased the hammer back, gently holding the trigger to muffle the sound of the action.

He saw a glint of starlight on metal between two buildings.

As he adjusted his eyes to the darkness and the dim light, he saw an arm move, and he thought he saw part of a man's leg sticking out.

He stopped and went into a semicrouch.

The arm moved and the reflected light surged along the barrel of a pistol.

The man was not coming out.

Slocum knew what he must do and he steeled himself to make the best of it. A few yards away, the jaws of death gaped open in the darkness. He could not see enough of Loomis to bring him down with a shot. There was only that arm and that leg, and the ugly snout of a pistol moving slowly to grab him in its sights.

Somehow, he thought, he must draw Loomis out in the open and still get the drop on him.

Slocum gritted his teeth and leaped from his crouch. He began to run on a parallel course to where Loomis was standing. Just as he started out, he heard the metallic snap of a pistol hammer as Loomis cocked his gun.

Perfect timing, Slocum thought and started his run in a zigzag pattern down the center of the street.

Behind him, he heard Linda gasp, and it sounded like the panting of an animal in the stillness of the night.

13

Slocum knew that a man's vision changed during the night. If he was aiming a rifle or a pistol, the target would not be dead center in the gun sights. Instead, a shooter would have to aim higher or lower, depending upon distance and angle. He was counting on Loomis missing his first shot at a moving target and shooting either too high or too low.

His zigzag run would make him a harder target in the darkness.

Loomis cracked off a shot as soon as Slocum began his run.

There was a flash and a streak of orange fire that partially illuminated the shooter. The bullet whined as it caromed off a rock somewhere beyond Slocum.

Slocum fired at the flash as he headed toward it. He veered off after the pistol bucked and threw its lead. He heard it thunk into the dirt as he turned away. His boots thudded on the hard-packed dirt of the street and he crushed a wagon wheel rut into powder as Loomis fired off another shot. The lead whistled past him, a foot behind, and he heard it smack into an adobe storefront.

Slocum turned again and headed straight toward the ghostly cloud of smoke that rose above Loomis. He squeezed the trigger and felt the Colt come to life in his hand with its powerful explosion. A fiery lance spewed from the mouth of his pistol barrel, and the bullet hissed as it flew over three thousand feet per second.

Loomis stepped out from his hiding place. He held his pistol in two hands to steady his aim. But he swept the barrel over a running shadow, a black shadow that would not stand still. He cupped his left hand under his right, cradled his gun hand as he had practiced so many times firing at tin cans, paper targets, fence posts, and yucca trees. He spread his legs to steady himself and squinted his left eye as his right focused on the blade front sight and the running man who drew ever nearer, but dashed in a crooked line.

Slocum threw himself headlong into the dirt as Loomis squeezed off another shot. He heard the death whisper of the bullet as it passed above his head. He could not stop the thought that popped into his head, that if he had been standing, that lead pellet might have ripped into his balls, turning him into a gelding.

Slocum fired another shot at Loomis, then rolled to another position. He steadied the pistol barrel on Loomis, what he could see of him, and held his breath as he flexed his right index finger, depressing the trigger with a smooth gentle tug.

Loomis screamed as the first bullet tore a bloody chunk out of his left arm. He screamed again when Slocum's second bullet slammed into his gut with the force of a sixteen-pound iron maul, a sledgehammer blow that caved in his stomach and drove him backward a half foot. He felt the warm rush of blood as it flowed down his arm and out over his belt buckle. There was no pain at first, but his eyes blurred as he tried to strike back, to shoot the man lying facedown in the street, a puddle of ink on starlit dirt.

Slocum counted his shots. He had not reloaded after he shot Thorson, and he had fired three shots there in the street. Four cartridges. He had two left in the cylinder and one was under the hammer, lurking there like a demon of death, waiting for the hammer to strike its thin metal dome and explode it into being.

Loomis staggered out into the open, out of that space between hardened clay brick buildings. His legs wobbled and pain now seethed through to his brain like a fiery poison, a malevolent fluid that robbed him of his reflexes and his senses.

"Christ," Loomis gasped and tried to aim a pistol that floated back and forth in front of his eyes like something possessed of its own erratic will.

Slocum watched as Loomis lurched toward him. His jaw line hardened into steel and his eyes narrowed as he held the pistol steady, braced by his bipodal elbows. He aimed for a point in the middle of Loomis's chest and fired the Colt. Just a gentle steady squeeze. That was all that it took and the projectile was on its way, faster than the speed of sound, a whistling death that traveled faster than a thought.

Smack, the bullet crashed through Loomis's fragile breastplate, turning bone into splinters, ripping through an artery and gouging out a chunk of heart muscle, chewing it to a bloody pulp as it surged past, nipping off a portion of spine before blowing a hole the size of a man's folded fist in the center of Loomis's back.

His voice was gone, and in that last split second of consciousness, Loomis felt the light in his brain being snuffed out like a candle in a high wind. The light diminished to a pinpoint and then there was only blackness and a bottomless pit that was darker than the darkest night, deeper than the universe itself, and all feeling was gone. He toppled forward, a lifeless bag of useless bones and mortifying flesh. His body struck the ground with a thud, and his pistol twisted from his hand at a crazy angle.

There was the smell of burnt powder and wisps of smoke afloat like a fleeting mist that became part of the air, part of the night. Slocum's ears reverberated with the sounds of explosions and made him temporarily deaf. He got to his feet, with one bullet left in its cylinder, and walked over to Loomis's corpse. He towered above it as he pushed the slide and swung the cylinder out like a gate. He pushed the ramrod as he turned it from one click to another and each empty hull fell to the ground and made a brassy *tink* in the dirt.

He pushed fresh cartridges into the empty sleeves until his pistol's round magazine was full, then snapped the cylinder back into its niche between the barrel and the slot where the hammer fell. He looked around and listened.

Was there another shooter? Had Loomis been the only man sent to kill him?

He stepped away and melted into the shadows where Loomis had stood in ambush, that place of concealment that now felt like the hollowed-out earth of an open grave.

Curious people began to step onto the street on both sides of where he stood. Patrons from Chez Soleil cautiously stood in front of the café and peered up the street.

Slocum brushed the dirt off the front of his clothes and stepped out. He headed for where he had left Linda. He found her leaning in an empty doorway.

"Did you kill him?" she asked.

"Yes."

"It was Loomis, wasn't it?"

"Yes."

"I never did like that little toady," she said. "You know he won't quit. He'll send Morgan Sombra after you, and Gustav Adler, another gunman in Willie's employ. Gustav is pure mean and Sombra is as snaky as they come."

"Obadiah told me about Adler and I've met Sombra."

"John, let's get out of here," she said. "Do you have something to drink in your saddlebags?"

"Matter of fact, I do. Some fine Kentucky bourbon bought in Santa Fe."

"I have a stomach full of butterflies. I heard someone tell someone else to go and fetch the sheriff."

"We'll have to go by the saloon, where my horse is hitched."

"Can I ride double?"

"You bet," he said.

They walked through the sparse crowd of gawkers back to the Socorro Saloon. Slocum helped Linda step up and take a seat behind the cantle. He mounted up and she clung to him as he turned Ferro onto the street. Swain walked toward them.

"I was just coming to get our horses," he said. "The rooming house has a small stable right behind it. Your room is ready, John."

"Want us to wait for you?" Slocum asked.

"No, you go on. I heard shots a while ago. Close to the rooming house."

"Rabbits," Slocum said.

"He shot Ruben Loomis," Linda blurted out. "Scroggs sent him to kill John."

"Ah, did you kill him, John?"

"He wasn't moving. And he wasn't breathing."

"Good riddance. You watch your back, John. There's more where he came from."

"I know. Adler and Sombra."

"Two that we know of," Swain said enigmatically.

"Did you get your business done?"

"Some of it," Swain said. "I'll finish up in the morning. Breakfast? They have a little dining hall at the rooming house."

"What time?"

"Oh, an hour or so after daybreak."

"I'll meet you there," Slocum said.

"We'll meet you there," Linda said emphatically and squeezed Slocum's waist with both arms.

"A threesome then," Swain said, and touched a finger to his hat brim in farewell.

Slocum rode down the street. Linda put her head against his shoulder.

"I'm glad to be with you," she whispered.

"I'm glad you're staying the night. Socorro seems to be a dangerous place at night."

She laughed, a feeble titter that tickled his ear.

"I feel safe with you," she said.

After he put Ferro up in the stable and stripped him of saddle, bridle, saddlebags, and bedroll, with its double-barrel shotgun swathed inside it, he and Linda went into the rooming house. The clerk handed him his key after Slocum signed the register. He was a balding, gray-haired man in his sixties, with a day's gray beard stubble on his chin, bright red suspenders, and horn-rimmed glasses with thick lenses.

"No loud singin' or boisterous conversation or noise after eleven," he said.

"We'll be as quiet as a couple of mice," Slocum said.

"'Night," the clerk said, then affixed a green eyeshade to his head and sat down at the desk, adjusting the lamp wick to give him more light. He was reading *Huckleberry Finn* by Mark Twain.

Slocum unlocked the door to Room 3 on the ground

floor and entered to find a lamp already lit. There was a large brass bed against the wall, a table, two chairs, and a small sofa in the center. Next to the bed there was a wardrobe and, against the opposite wall, a bureau with a pitcher of water, glasses, and a chamber pot tucked under its wooden bottom.

"All the comforts of home," Linda said as she patted the cotton comforter atop the bed. There were some Currier & Ives prints in frames on the walls, small scenes of New York with horses and hansoms and leafy trees.

Slocum set the bedroll on the floor next to the wardrobe and slung his saddlebags over the back of a chair. He reached in and pulled out a bottle of Old Kentucky bourbon that was 100 proof.

He dug out a tin cup from his saddlebag as Linda went to the bureau and filled two glasses half-full of water.

"I have only one cup for the bourbon," he said. "I'll swig from the bottle."

"We could both swig from the bottle," she said. "After all, we'll be kissing each other."

"Will we?"

"Passionately," she said as she sat down and placed the water glasses on the table, one for her, and one for Slocum, opposite each other.

He pulled the cork from the bottle with his teeth, poured bourbon into the cup, and handed it to her. He set the bottle down and sat.

She sniffed the liquid in her cup.

Closed her eyes.

"Umm. It smells so nice. Makes me think of hayfields and woods full of oak trees and black walnuts, an old silo, and a field of wheat."

"Kentucky is a fine place for all those things," he said. He lifted the bottle, tilted it, and drank a swallow. She held the cup to her lips, smelled the aroma, and drank a sip.

"It tastes like it smells," she said, and there was promise in her voice, a cat's purr of contentment, a smoky sinuousness that slinked through her voice like a prowling cougar.

"What is it like to kill a man?" she asked abruptly.

"What?"

"How do you feel when you take the life of another man? Do you feel guilt? Remorse? Anger? Regret?"

He looked off at the window, then tilted his head and examined the ceiling. But he was looking beyond those things, looking inside himself. He was searching for memory, for feelings that he had discarded like worn-out shoes or crumpled up like paper and thrown in a wastebasket.

"The first time I killed a man," he said, "it felt like the earth had dropped out from under me. It felt like I was in an elevator and the ropes had been slashed. I felt as if I were falling through a trapdoor, or from a high cliff."

"My, that's interesting," she said. "What about tonight? You shot and killed two men. How did you feel when you did it?"

She leaned forward and he saw that she was genuinely interested in his answer.

"Tonight," he said, "was different. When I was a boy, there was a mean dog that came onto our place in Georgia and he chased me and he bit my ankles. I started carrying a stick, and when this dog snarled and ragged me, I hit him, drove him off. That's how I felt with the Swede. He was a vicious dog out to chew me up. My gun was a stick and I beat him off."

"And Loomis?"

"One time, up in the Rockies, I was hunted by a hungry wolf. I had killed an elk and was packing some of the meat back to camp. The smell was enough to attract this big timber wolf. He came after me, snarling and baring his fangs. I tried to shoo him away, but he went for my throat. I pulled out my pistol and shot him in midair. That bastard was at least nine feet long from tail tip to muzzle. Black as night. He was a beautiful animal and I hated to kill it. But it was me or him. That's how I felt about Loomis. Hiding in the dark, trying to put out my lamp. A wolf on the prowl. I didn't shoot a man, Linda. I shot a coward who put his life on the line when he came after me. He expected to win. He lost."

Linda was silent for several seconds.

"I think I want you to make love to me," she said, and there was a husk in her voice that was like a woman in season. He felt the breath of her lust on his face and a tickle in his loins as if she had touched his manhood with one of her fingernails.

"Do you want to finish your drink first?" he said, and the words fought through his throat to emerge in that same kind of husk, a raspy series of voluble vowels and consonants that were an invitation to bed him in some ancient and forbidden garden.

To his surprise, she upended her cup and downed the whiskey without so much as a blink of an eye.

He corked the bottle and rose from his chair.

"Do you want me to put out the lamp?" he asked as she arose and walked to the bed, began to slip out of her dress.

"No," she said. "I want to see your face when you lie on top of me. I want to see your body and what you do when I touch you."

"Modesty becomes you," he said, and she laughed.

"I want you to see me, too," she said, and slipped out of her panties. She sat on the bed and removed her shoes and let them fall with a pair of thunks. She was all slender legs and trim ankles and delicate hands and wrists, and her breasts were sculptures fashioned by a master artist, her hair like flowing silk down her back over comely shoulders and the smooth expanse of womanly flesh.

He almost gasped at her beauty, and for a long moment, he stood there so enraptured he could not move.

When he did move, he was like a man on fire, divesting himself of flaming garments until he stood as naked as Adam before the Fall, and there, waiting for him, was Eve with her forbidden fruit, just waiting for him, as calm and beautiful as a Siren on a sea rock waiting for his ship to float in close.

He took her in his arms and they kissed.

The world dropped away into the night, and the soft breeze caressed them as they came together and became a single image known only to lovers and a night full of stars and drifting planets.

14

Linda was warm and sinewy as Slocum clasped her in his arms. Body to body. Lips to lips. They devoured each other with the pure energy of passion. A lambent fire built between them until both writhed with desire. His tongue ventured into her mouth and she undulated under his caress as if she were impaled on the spit of his manhood.

Linda reached down and grasped his cock. She squeezed it with a gentle tenderness that sent shoots of pleasure through his loins and up his spine as if his entire body was consumed by an icy wave that burned hot by the time the sensation reached his brain.

"Oh, oh," she moaned, and Slocum slid a hand down to her nest, probed through the wiry hairs that guarded the portal to her sex, and slid a finger into that warm wet cunny where desire beckoned like some hungry mouth. He rubbed his fingertip over the crown of her clitoris and she buckled under him. Her legs spread wide and he probed her with his finger until she squirmed and cried out, "There, there, oh yes, John, right there."

She squeezed his cock and it throbbed in her fingers like a bird beating its wings against a cage. His temples pulsed with the pressure of her hand and she thrashed against him as an electric orgasm surged through her body, through every fiber of her being.

"Oh, John," she cried, "now, now. Take me now."

He withdrew his hand at her hot wet portal and mounted her, thrusting his cock into her with unerring accuracy. He slid deep, brushing over the tingle of her clit, and felt her body push against his, her cunt grasping him in a muscular grip and squeezing, squeezing as her hips undulated in an ancient rhythm that knew no boundaries of race or creed.

"Sweet," he murmured as he plunged still deeper into the warm moist honeycomb of her sex. "So damned sweet."

"That's it," she breathed. "Go deep, John, go deep."

He rose and fell, loin to loin, his cock a smooth driving piston into her pulsating, grasping purse, rubbing against her clit and making her buck beneath him like a galloping mare.

She tightened her embrace around his back, and he felt the sharp pressure of her fingertips as she buried them in his flesh.

Golden lamplight flayed their shadows against the wall, delicate whips that transformed their movements into a dark ballet performed in slow motion. Shadows flowed into shadows and light flitted like large fireflies in a spinning cascade of fluid searchlights, dazzling stars that had come to the earth in masquerade, ever moving, ever changing, ever challenging the shades of their beings dancing on the wall, the glassy windowpane.

"Don't come yet," she whispered, her whisper a gasp laden with the throaty husk of desire.

"No," he said. "Not yet. It's too good, Linda. Too damned good."

"Yes, it's wonderful," she breathed and gave herself up to him, relaxing her fingers digging into his back, and swabbing him with her hands, sliding over his hips and up his sides as if she were a blind person seeking to identify the lover at her loins.

"Precious," she said. Her voice was soft and the word held a meaning only for herself, but Slocum felt the weight of it as her hips rose to meet his and he plunged to the very depths of her womb, his cock basking in the warm flow of her honey, his nostrils filled with the musk of her womanly scent.

"So precious," she said again.

He slowed his rhythmic thrusts and drew pleasure from her as smoke through a pipe stem. Slow and deep. Slow and deep. Until she was clawing at him like a woman gone insane, screaming softly and begging him for more with every snail-slow thrust.

"Ooooh, you do it so good, John," she said, and her hips rose to meet him on the downward thrust until he held fast inside her, feeling the heat of her surge through him like flame-warmed fleece.

Linda gave back as much as she was given, and Slocum felt their vibrations meld together as if they were one person, joined together below the waist. He pumped in and out of her, but she matched his thrusts with upward jolts of her own, a perfect twin of himself, circus performers on a galloping steed, each in harmony with the other.

They did not speak for a long time as he prolonged his own orgasm to satisfy her. Her capacity for climaxes seemed to be limitless. She cried out each time her body rippled with a volcanic orgasm, and that emotional energy erupted from her body and blended into his.

"Oh, John," she cried out, and "Yes, John," and a stream of "ohs" burst from her throat as she soared ever higher on the throb-whip of ecstatic wings, a condor and an eagle, locked together in flight, cresting the tallest peaks with nearly every thrust of Slocum's driving bone into the moist hot pudding of her sex.

Finally, they both reached a plateau, some leveling off of need and desire, and he sensed that she was ready to finish this first segment of their lovemaking. His seed boiled in its sac, and it took all of his mental focus to keep it in check. But at last, he could hold back no longer.

"I'm going to come," he said, his voice a rasp of sound, a hoarse series of vocables from a throat squeezed tight with emotion.

"Yes, John, come, come, come inside me," she urged. "Blow your seed in me so that I can feel your soul."

He pumped up and down in a fury and pulled on her buttocks so that he buried his cock to the hilt. She screamed as he held her tight and his milky seed exploded from his scrotum and shot through his cock like a powerful jet from a fire hose. He felt it splash against the walls of her womb, and for that single long moment, they were both transported to the highest human pinnacle, a place where there was only the air of the gods. Time fell away like a discarded cloak, and in that single instant there was a glorious eternity, a feeling of immense power, of supreme mastery of time and space that stretched into infinity.

"Oh, God, yes," she breathed, and the voice was from another being, a woman floating in the high reaches of the rarified atmosphere far above the earth.

Slocum grunted as he spilled his seed and a supreme joy infused his body with a pleasure beyond measurement. It was that single moment when man was most godlike, beyond earthly emotions and desires. It was a moment never to be recaptured in memory, but forever indelible on the deepest part of the human soul.

He let her hips fall from his grasp and float to the bed, just as he and Linda floated downward from that great height where their emotions had carried them, floating like a pair of down feathers, weightless and satiated beyond simple satisfaction.

He fell out of her, limp and wet. He rolled from her body and lay at her side, all of his energy drained, all of his fires banked until they were on the coals of the afterglow, that seeping pleasure that soothed them like the comforting hand of a caring mother on the forehead of an ailing child.

"John," she said. "That was wonderful. You were wonderful."

"So were you, Linda."

"I feel you inside me, even though you have gone, John."

"I think that's what they call mating," he said. "Part of you is still with me and part of me is still with you. Hard to describe."

"You can't describe it," she said. "Neither can I. Nor can anyone."

"Maybe that's why we keep coming back for more," he said. "It's there, that great feeling, and then it's gone."

"Yes, it's gone, the part that is pitch perfect, that one moment when we both climax together. And then it's gone, just as the night goes with the coming of day."

"You put it real nice," he said.

"But still indescribable."

"Yes. You can't describe it. At least, I can't."

They lay there in a peaceful lassitude for several minutes, their hands on each other's smooth and damp stomachs, their perspiration drying in the coolness of the evening breeze through the open window.

"I'm going to light a cheroot," he said. "Want one?"

"I'll draw a puff or two on yours, if you let me."

"Sure," he said, and slid from the bed. He got a cigar, bit off the end and spat it out, struck a match, and carried an ashtray to the bedside table.

She raised her head and he passed the cheroot to her. She took a small puff, but did not inhale.

"Good," she said.

"You liar," he said.

They both laughed and Slocum leaned back against the pillow and smoked alone as Linda lay beside him, content as any kitten with a belly full of warm milk.

"Tell me about your uncle," he said later. "Did you know he was coming to Socorro?"

"No, I didn't know he was coming. But I'm not surprised, knowing Willie like I do. Maggots seem to be attracted to filth, and my uncle is a worm of the first rank."

"But he's your father's brother."

"My father hated his brother. Hated him for what he stood for, for what he did."

"Is your father still alive?"

"No, he died two years ago. He had a cancer. My mother died the year before. Daddy missed her. He didn't die peaceful. He was in great pain and yet he never complained. He was a man. A man's man. Unlike my Uncle Hiram. A man like you, John."

"I'd like to have known him," he said.

"You would have liked him. He would have liked you, I think."

"Well, we'll never know."

"Maybe. Maybe we can know some things without knowing."

"You mean . . ."

"I mean that some things we have to take on faith,

John." She reached over and squeezed his limp penis. "And some things," she said, "we can see and touch and feel."

"If you keep touching me like that, Linda, you'll never get a wink of sleep. Nor will I."

"Sleep is for mortals," she said. "You and I are gods."

They made love again, with the lamp blown out and moonlight shining in the window and filling the room with a soft silvery light, granting the room a special glow that came from far away, from the distant realm of the gods.

15

As soon as Slocum had left the saloon with Linda and Swain, Willie Scroggs had flown into a rage. The big Swede was dead, cut down by a stranger's bullets. Thorson's lifeless face was sallow, drained of blood, and there was a black hole in his forehead that was turning purple at the edges.

Wu Chen stood next to Hiram Littlepage. He held a white handkerchief to his nose. Thorson's sphincter muscle had relaxed and he had voided himself when he died so suddenly.

Scroggs cursed under his breath. The two bartenders leaned over the bar top to stare at Thorson's body. Ruben Loomis had returned to the bar once he saw Slocum saunter away, and now the hired gunman stood a few feet away, a blank expression on his face. Scroggs looked over at him.

"Did you get a good look at that man who shot the Swede?" Scroggs asked.

Loomis nodded.

"I want you to get that bastard," Scroggs said. "Track

him down. Shoot him. Back or front, it don't make no difference."

"Yes, sir," Loomis said, and turned to leave the saloon.

Miranda and her daughter, Maria Luisa, were like two hawks. They watched and listened. They stood somewhat apart from the other woman who worked at the saloon.

"That man," Maria Luisa whispered to her mother in Spanish, "he was with Jethro's brother."

"I know," Miranda said.

"Do you know his name?"

"No, but he is very strong. Very fast with the pistol."

"Yes, I saw it all. I saw how fast he was and how he shot the Swedish man. I am worried about Jethro."

"Do not worry. The brother—he is called Obadiah, no?—he is very strong, too. I saw him speak to Scroggs and I think he gave Scroggs a warning."

"Still, I worry. Scroggs wishes to kill the tall stranger, the man who wears the black clothes. That is why he sends Loomis to kill him."

"Perhaps the stranger will kill Loomis, or perhaps Obadiah will shoot him."

"I do not like that Loomis man."

"Nor do I," Miranda said.

Scroggs looked over at the two bartenders, who still gawked at Thorson.

"Eddie, get some boys to clean up this mess," he said. "Take the Swede out back and send somebody over to Parmenter's. Tell him to bring his wagon."

"Parmenter is the undertaker, I presume," Littlepage said.

"Yeah, old Josh Parmenter cuts 'em and guts 'em, plants 'em at Boot Hill in a pine box six feet under. A damned bandit, that's what he is. But he's all we've got here in Socorro."

"When you get finished giving orders, I'll take a look at that basement you've been telling me about," Littlepage said.

Scroggs held up a hand, looked over at Cal, who was back at his job, pulling beer for the patrons sitting at the bar once again.

"Cal, can you find somebody to fetch Gustav over here and maybe find out where Shadow is?"

"I'll see what I can do," Cal said.

"Do it," Scroggs snapped. "And somebody better tell Paddy Degnan to get his ass over here."

"I'll send Freddie after the sheriff," Cal said. "Where is he? Upstairs?"

"Yep. Freddie knows where Degnan hangs his hat."

"I'm right on it, boss," Cal said.

He spoke to men at the bar and two of them left their places and went to pick up Thorson's body.

"Let's you and I take a look at my basement, Hiram," Scroggs said with one last look of disgust at the body of Thorson.

The two men walked to the back and down a hall. Small globe oil lamps attached to the wall every four feet provided illumination. They entered a small room off to the side where, besides some shelves, on one of which sat several oil lanterns and lamps, there was only a large trapdoor with a braided rope handle.

Light from the hall sprayed through the open doorway. Scroggs picked up a box of matches off the shelf and lifted the glass chimney of a lamp. He struck the match and lit the wick, turned it up.

"Follow me," he said to Littlepage.

Scroggs lifted the trapdoor and let it fall against a wooden stanchion. There was a gaping square hole in the floor and steps leading down into the basement. There was a round wooden rail on one wall of the stairs, and Scroggs guided himself downward into the black maw of the basement, his and Littlepage's shadows large against the earthen wall, shadows that moved like black leviathans flowing down into an inky sea.

Lanterns and lamps hung from the wooden beams within easy reach. The lamp in Scroggs's hand threw the whitewashed walls into relief. The room was large and possessed several straight chairs, a couple of stools, and two long rustic tables. Scroggs set the lamp on one of the tables. Littlepage walked around the room, a slight smile on his face, as if he was imagining tapestries on the walls, plush rugs on the floor and sofas, pillows and soft pads on the dirt floor.

"Well, what do you think, Hiram?" Scroggs asked when Littlepage returned to the table.

"This will do fine. I want Wu Chen to see it. He knows how to decorate such a place."

"Decorate?"

"Cushions and exotic rugs on the walls and floor, plush pillows, places to put the hookahs, a cabinet to store bottles of water, and of course, a safe to store the opium."

"And you think folks will come down to this dungeon?"

"Once they taste the evil flower, they will kill to come to this place," Littlejohn said.

"And we'll make a lot of money, you say."

"A lot of money."

"I'll go up and get Wu Chen. I want to hear what he has to say. "

"It does not concern you, Wilbur. I will pay for all that we need. You provide the room. Wu Chen and I will furnish the room and the opium."

Littlepage rubbed his hands together.

Scroggs climbed the stairs. He returned in a few minutes with Wu Chen, who descended the stairs timidly.

"Look around, Wu Chen," Littlepage said, "and see what we need."

"It is a large room," Wu Chen said as he walked the perimeters of the room. "It is very dark. That is good. Very quiet and peaceful."

"How soon can you bring the pillows and the hookahs?" Littlepage asked.

"My wagon is full," Wu Chen said.

"And do you have enough opium?"

"Yes. Quite enough."

"Then we're set, Wilbur," Littlepage said. "After you close tonight, you give me two strong men to help Wu Chen and we will transform this basement into a paradise for opium smokers."

"The patrons don't eat the opium?" Scroggs asked.

Littlepage shook his head.

"Smoking is faster. We can also turn the powder into a fluid and use hypodermic needles to inject the drug into the bloodstream of those who are in the iron grip of the drug. Isn't that so, Wu Chen?" Littlepage looked at Wu Chen, whose eyes glittered in the yellowish glow of the lamp.

"They do not escape the dragon's claws," Wu Chen said. "We will make much money."

"How do we get people to try the opium?" Scroggs asked.

"Pick them one by one," Littlejohn said. "Invite them down to this place of magic. Tell them you are going to let them smoke a kind of cigar or cigarette that will take away all their pains and make them a little bit drunk."

"And you think they will smoke the opium? The men who come to my saloon are mostly ignorant Mexes. They are dumb as a sack full of doornails."

"The Mexicans are the ones who will fall to the clutches of opium the quickest, Wilbur. Many of them have smoked marijuana. They have floated on the smoke from those little brown cigarettes. They will float higher with the opium. Isn't that so, Wu Chen?"

"Oh, yes," Wu Chen said. "The Mexicans love the opium. They love the dreams."

"The Mexicans will rob for you, Wilbur. They will kill for you. Just to have money to buy opium. It is magic. And do not forget the ladies, the women in this town. Once they taste the petals of the poppy, they will demand it. They will beg their husbands and their lovers to bring them here so that they can float like eagles and dream of paradise."

Scroggs smiled as he listened to Littlepage's rhapsodic promises. He envisioned the room filled with paying customers who would never be able to resist the opium. Just like Jethro Swain, only more so.

He walked up to Littlepage and extended his hand. The two men shook hands. Wu Chen shook Scroggs's hand as well.

"You will be very happy with the success of this venture," Littlepage said.

"I agree," Wu Chen said.

With that, the deal was sealed. The three men ascended the stairs. At the top, Scroggs blew out the lamp and placed it back on the shelf.

"Now," Littlepage said, "all you have to do is kill that man who shot the Swedish man. No one must stand in your way."

They entered the saloon. A couple of the women were scrubbing the blood from the floor, and Cal was sprinkling sawdust from a bucket onto the remainder of the bloodstains. Scroggs was glad to see that the men were drinking again. They had returned to their tables and some stood or sat at the bar. There was conversation and the ring of the cash register. More people had streamed into the saloon, as word of the killing had spread.

"Nothing draws a crowd like violence and death," Scroggs said to Littlepage.

"That is why I like Socorro," Littlepage said. "The men can bring their guns in here and there is always the chance one of those pistols will go off and draw blood and life."

"Not many shootings in here," Scroggs said. "But we do have some pretty good fights."

"Perhaps you should schedule a public hanging in here every now and then," Littlepage joked.

"Not a bad idea, Hiram," Scroggs said. "Let's drink to that, and the success of, what do you call that place where they smoke from those glass hookers?"

"Hookahs," Littlepage corrected, "and most people call such places 'opium dens.' They are private lairs where mice are turned into lions."

"An opium den," Scroggs mouthed as he led Wu Chen and Littlepage to his customary table, holding his hand up with three fingers extended when he caught Cal's eye.

Just as he and the other two men sat down, he saw the batwing doors swing open. Sheriff Degnan and Morgan Sombra strode in like a pair of gamecocks entering the ring to do battle.

Scroggs smiled and waited for Degnan and Sombra to come to his table.

He felt like a great lord, master of his domain, his castle, which would soon have a dungeon full of opium smoke and the heady aroma of money.

16

Paddy Degnan walked over to speak with Cal Meecham, Sombra at his heels.

"Where's Olaf's body?"

"Out in the back," Cal answered.

"When Josh Parmenter comes in, have him pick up the Swede."

"Where's Eddie?" Cal asked.

"He's with Parmenter."

"How come?" Cal asked.

"He stayed to help with the corpse of Loomis," the sheriff replied.

Sombra stood there, somber-faced, a slight tic playing with the muscles of his jawbone. His eyes were as dull as cloudy marbles covered in dust, and he had a thumb tucked behind his gun belt as if he was ready to spring into action at any moment.

Degnan was all coiled up inside, like a spring. A Mexican shopkeeper had knocked on his door and told him that a man had been shot over on Palo Verde Street. He and Sombra had ridden over there and found Loomis. He had questioned all the bystanders while Sombra went to fetch the undertaker. Nobody saw the shooting. Nobody knew who had killed Loomis. But he had his suspicions, and so did Morgan Sombra.

"Eddie said Slocum shot the Swede. That so?"

"I don't know what the man's name was. Tall, dressed in black. Very fast with a gun." Cal swabbed the bar top with a grimy towel, stopped rubbing when he finished talking.

"That was Slocum," Degnan said.

"You see Wilcox?" Cal asked.

"No. Why?"

"I sent him to fetch Parmenter."

"Well, he's probably running around in the dark out there like a lost dog. He ain't got the brains of a toy whistle, that one."

"Yeah," Cal said and slapped the towel on another part of the bar.

Degnan and Sombra walked to the back table where Scroggs and Littlepage sat.

"You shouldn't have sent Loomis after Slocum," he said as he sat down. Sombra sat next to him, as silent as stone.

"I sent him after the man who killed Olaf," Scroggs said.

"Well, you got Loomis killed," Degnan said.

"What?" Scroggs reared back in his seat.

"You heard me. Loomis is dead. Parmenter's got him in the Black Maria. On his way here to pick up Thorson's corpse."

"Shit," Scroggs said.

"Did you know Slocum's a wanted man? Got a price on his head?"

"Yeah. Morg told me. I told Olaf to put Slocum's lamp

out and he walked into a bullet. Shit, I never saw nobody draw and shoot that fast."

"Well, if you saw that, you should have just sat tight and not sent Loomis to his death."

"I figured Loomis was man enough and smart enough not to face that jasper down."

"Well, he wasn't," Degnan said. "People heard a lot of shots, but nobody saw a damned thing."

"But you know it was Slocum who killed Ruben?"

"Who else? You sent Loomis to kill Slocum, like you sent Thorson to kill him. Now, both men are dead as door-nails and Slocum's walking around free as a fucking bird."

"Have a drink, Paddy," Scroggs said.

"I just might."

"Morg, you want to wet your whistle?" Scroggs asked. "You ain't goin' to find Slocum tonight. Unless you know where he's cribbed."

"I don't know," Sombra said.

"And I don't know neither," Degnan said. "We'll both have a drink and then I got to get some shut-eye afore mornin'. I'll get that bastard Slocum."

Degnan looked at Sombra.

"Or Morgan will. He's plumb primed to blow a hole in that sonofabitch.

"I don't believe I've met this gentleman," Degnan said, glancing at Littlepage.

Scroggs introduced Littlepage to Degnan and Sombra.

"I seen this Chinese man here before," Degnan said.

"Wu Chen," Scroggs said.

"He don't say much, do he?" Degnan commented.

"I only speak when it is necessary," Wu Chen said in his lilting Chinese accent.

"You sell opium to Willie here, I think," Degnan said.

"When he wishes," Wu Chen said.

Littlepage stood up.

"Willie, Wu Chen and I have much to do. I'll see you later."

Wu Chen also got up. The two left the table and walked through the batwing doors.

"Littlepage," Degnan said. "Any relation to Linda?"

"He's her uncle. And no love lost between them, I gather," Scroggs said.

"Not much resemblance either. I don't see her nowhere."

"She left with Slocum and that bastard Obadiah Swain," Scroggs said.

A waiter stopped by with glasses and a full bottle of whiskey, set them on the table. He drifted away without speaking, and there was once again a wide berth around Scroggs's table.

"I guess I can check at Linda's house," Degnan said. "I know where she lives. Maybe she took Slocum home with her."

"I wouldn't know," Scroggs said.

"I know where she lives, too," Sombra said. "You want me to check?"

Degnan thought about it for a two-second moment.

"You know his horse, Morg. You can ride by her place and see if it's tied up there, I reckon."

"I'll do that," Sombra said. "Soon as I finish my drink."

"You going to shoot him in bed?" Scroggs asked. "You might get two birds with one stone."

"Makes no difference to me," Sombra said. "If I have to shoot Slocum through a pretty woman, well, that's just the way the cards play out."

"That would be murder," Scroggs said, still teasing Sombra.

"Not in my book, it wouldn't," Degnan said, and poured himself a drink.

Sombra lit a cigarette and drank his whiskey. He was in no hurry. If Slocum was at Linda Littlepage's, he would be there most of the night.

He didn't trust Linda any more than he trusted any woman. Especially any woman in Socorro.

Scroggs looked at Sombra. He knew how dangerous a man he was. If anyone could kill Slocum, he would pick Morgan.

Sombra, he thought, was pure killer, through and through. He had no conscience, no morals, no faith in anything but himself. And if he killed a pretty woman in bed with Slocum, he wouldn't even blink an eye.

Sombra would probably laugh. And gloat.

"Here's to the death of Slocum," Scroggs said, raising his glass. He clinked it against those of Degnan and Sombra.

"Here's to Slocum," Degnan said. "Soon may he die."

The three men laughed and the smoke from Sombra's cigarette swirled over the table like some wraith, twisting in the light from the lamps like a gilded snake.

17

Linda and Slocum met Obie Swain for breakfast in the lobby of the rooming house. The twin doors to the small dining room were open, and the aromas of coffee and food were semaphores to the three, wafting messages to their nostrils and stirring the juices in their stomachs.

"Hungry?" Swain asked.

"Famished," Linda said.

"I could eat," Slocum said.

"Well, let's set down to a table in there," Swain said. "I could eat the south end of a northbound buffalo."

They walked into the dining room, where a few early patrons sat at tables covered with red-and-white-checkered tablecloths, forking food into their mouths, drinking water from glasses, and talking in low conversational tones so that the room buzzed with snatches of insect speech pitched too low to comprehend, but amiable and intimate as was appropriate at that early hour.

"My tummy's growling like a lion," Linda whispered to

Slocum as a waiter showed them to a table by a window that looked out onto the street.

"My lion could eat your lion right now," he said. "Smells good."

"Ummm," she murmured.

"Is this table to your liking?" the white-aproned waiter asked as he pulled out a chair for Linda.

"Perfect," Swain said, and Slocum let him take the lead.

"Put this on one bill," Swain told the waiter, a stoop-shouldered man in his forties with thin brown hair that held a sheen, white shirt and string tie, neatly pressed dark gab-ardine trousers, and polished shoes with new leather soles that creaked when he walked. "And give the bill to me."

"Yes, sir. My name is Corly and here is a menu of this morning's fare." He handed Swain a handwritten parchment-like sheet that bore a list of food items with prices in bold, cursive numbers placed at the end of the meal descriptions.

"Well, they got hen fruit and ham, cornmeal mush and flapjacks," Swain said. "What's your pleasure?"

Linda scanned the menu. "Eggs and ham will do just fine," she said.

"Biscuits?" Swain asked.

"Yes, with a little honey, if they have it."

"I'm going to have me the same, with some of that red-eye gravy and flapjacks," Swain said.

"Sounds good to me," Slocum said.

Corly returned and took their order. He set glasses on the table and filled them with water.

"I'm afraid I won't be able to stay long after breakfast, Obie." Linda said. "I've much to do, and a cat and a dog to tend to. But thank you for breakfast."

"Mighty sorry to hear that, Linda," Swain said.

"I'll walk you home," Slocum said.

"No, please don't. I don't live far and I love to walk in

the morning. You stay, John. You have things to do. Right, Obie?"

"I've already saddled John's horse," he said. "And mine. We have some miles to go, I'm afraid."

"See?" she said to Slocum.

Slocum felt trapped. Obie seemed to be in charge of his life at the moment. He would rather have walked Linda home, sealed a friendship that was already past the budding stage and was about to blossom.

"I guess I'd better ride with Obie," he said, and tried to avoid the lameness of the statement. But there was defeat in his tone. Linda patted his hand in understanding and he felt better after that. He melted inside under the bright warmth of her smile.

The breakfast arrived, and the two men ate and talked while they forked flapjacks, fried eggs, and ham chunks into their mouths. Linda listened to them, but did not offer any remarks. When she was finished, she arose from her chair.

"I must go," she said.

She leaned down and kissed Slocum on the forehead.

"Good-bye, John," she said. "I hope to see you again very soon. Thank you for a wonderful evening."

"I hate to see you go, Linda. I'm very fond of you."

"Sorry," she said.

The two men watched her walk through the dining room and out into the lobby. In moments, she was gone.

"I'm not going to say anything, John," Swain said.

"Good. Neither am I."

"I finished my business in town, John," Swain said. "I got a dozen sticks of DuPont sixty/forty and enough fuses and blasting caps to get the job done."

"You going to blast a new mine?"

"No, it's an old one. But I found something the other

day and I want to go deeper into the mountain. Might find more of it."

"What did you find?" Slocum asked.

Swain reached into his pocket and pulled out a dirty green stone, oblong in shape, with a few crevices in its unshined surface. He laid it on the table in front of Slocum. Slocum picked it up.

"That's turquoise," Swain said. "There's more of it. A lot more, I think, but I have a small basket full of stones just like that."

"What's it worth?"

"Plenty," Swain said. "I might make more money from turquoise than I do from the silver I'm mining."

Slocum put the stone back down and pushed it across the table.

Swain picked it up, put it back in his pocket.

"The name of the stone has something to do with Turkey," Swain said. "The name means 'Turkish,' I think. It's fairly rare from what I found out at the assay office. At least in these parts."

"Good luck," Slocum said. He sipped his coffee, then lit up a cheroot. Swain lit a cigar and the two men smoked as Corly cleared away theirs and Linda's plates.

"Will there be anything else, gentlemen?" the waiter asked.

"No, just bring me the bill, Corly," Swain said.

Then he turned to Slocum as the waiter walked away with the tray of dishes.

"Want to ride out to my digs with me, John?"

"Now?"

"That's where I'm headed after I look in on Jethro and Penny."

"You trust me that much? Seems to me that Scroggs is

determined to find where you live and rob you and your mine."

"I never return home the same way twice, John. And yeah, I trust you."

"Do you know what happened last night after Linda and I left the French place?"

"I know someone put Loomis's lamp out. I figured it was you."

"It was."

"Bushwhacked you, did he?"

Slocum nodded and blew smoke into the air.

"Well, Scroggs will send Shadow after you, that's for damned sure."

"I'll keep an eye out."

"He has another gunslinger who's just as mean and treacherous as Sombra. I told you about him."

"The German?"

"Yeah. Gustav Adler. You want to watch out for him, too. He's just as sneaky as Shadow. And he's pretty good at back shootin'. Just like Sombra. Willie Scroggs knows how to pick 'em, that's for damned sure."

"I reckon they both can stop a bullet same as Loomis and Thorson."

Swain laughed in his throat, and took another puff from his cigar. Then he poked it into his coffee cup and they both heard it hiss as the tip drowned in the dark liquid.

Corly returned and presented the bill. Swain paid in silver and gave the waiter a modest gratuity.

"Thank you, sir," Corly said.

"Let's be off, then, John," Swain said as he rose from his chair. "Get your gear and I'll meet you out front. Hotel bill's paid."

"Thanks, Obie. Your generosity knows no bounds."

"Oh, it knows bounds, all right, but I'm grateful to you for saving Jethro's life and takin' care of Penny, seein' them both safely home."

"What I did for your brother and your niece requires no gratitude on your part, Obie." He got up from the table. "I'll see you out front in a few minutes."

The two men walked to the lobby. Swain went out the back door to the stables, while Slocum went to his room and picked up his belongings.

Swain was waiting for him in front of the rooming house. Ferro was stamping his right foot and pawing the ground. He whinnied when he saw Slocum.

"He's been grained and brushed," Swain said. "Curried him some myself early this morning."

"You've got the heart of a saint, Obie," Slocum said as he tied on his bedroll and set his saddlebags, slid his Winchester into its scabbard.

"Saint, no," Swain said. "You've got a fine horse and I admire good horseflesh."

Slocum swung himself up in the saddle.

"Lead on, Macduff," he said.

Swain chuckled.

"You admire Shakespeare, John. Same as I do."

"I've seen some of his plays. The man has a gift for the English tongue."

"I don't understand half of it, but it's sure pretty to listen to."

The two men rode out of Socorro and took a different route from what Slocum remembered.

The sun's rim had cleared the horizon and there were opal clouds in the east, at their backs, small cottony puffs that seemed to have been painted in pastels. The bleak and rocky, cactus-strewn landscape stretched out ahead of them, all pink and rosy as one of Homer's dawns, with a deep stillness except for the muffled sound of the horses' hooves as they rode at a leisurely pace over unmarked ground.

Slocum finished his cheroot and crushed it out against the sole of his boot before he tossed it to the ground.

"You leave a trail that way," Swain observed.

"I've left many that way."

"Unlikely anyone out here will read it."

"Let's hope," Slocum said.

"Yeah, let's do," Swain said.

He kept looking back as they rode in a wide circle. Slocum was surprised when he spotted Jethro's and Penny's adobe home, lying not in front of them, but below them.

Swain reined up and Slocum stopped beside him.

They stayed there for several minutes, then one of the Mexicans stepped from the shadow of the stables and waved.

"We can go down there now," Swain said. "That was Carlos Jimenez sayin' all was well."

"That's good to know," Slocum said.

"Juan and Carlos are both reliable men."

Slocum said nothing. The sun was bright in his eyes and he pulled his hat brim down. He sniffed the morning air and caught his own scent.

He wondered if Penny would be able to smell Linda's musk all over his body. Or would she just smell the medicine reek in her home?

Funny, he thought, to be worried about what a woman would think about him. But Penny was special, just as Linda was. He was grateful to both and beholden to neither.

18

Gustav Adler wore two pistols, each with ivory grips. He was nearly six feet tall, with flaxen hair and pale blue eyes as cold as glacier ice. He stood there in the basement room with Scroggs, whose expression was one of unbridled delight. Adler's face was impassive and his cold eyes betrayed nothing of his feelings.

"Well, what do you think, Gus?" Scroggs asked.

Wu Chen was fluffing up a red satin pillow the size of a wagon wheel in one corner of the room. Littlepage sat on a plush chair, legs sprawled out, his hat tilted back on his head. He bore a look of satisfaction on his lean face.

"It looks like a Chink whorehouse," Adler said.

"A place you ain't never been, Gus."

"That is so, Willie, but if I had gone to one, in Frisco, it would look like this, with all them fancy rugs and the burnin' incense."

There were brass incense burners placed strategically around the room. There was a small golden glow in each and a plume of smoke emerging from the small holes in the top.

"I didn't call you down here to scuttle what Wu Chen has done to this hole in the ground, Gus. This room, this den, is going to afford me the chance to finish building my hotel next to the saloon. That incense is soon goin' to smell just like money."

"Haw," Adler snorted. "Ain't nobody but Chinks goin' to eat your opium, Willie."

"Not countin' Wu Chen there, you won't find a Chink within a thousand miles of Socorro."

"Yeah. That is what I mean, Willie. White folks ain't goin' to chew on opium."

"They'll smoke it, Gus. That's what all them glass bowls with water in 'em and them tubes is for. For smokin'."

Adler snorted in derision again, which irritated Scroggs. He stabbed Adler with a lancing look that showed his disapproval of the German's assessment of the basement opium den.

"My opinion, Willie," Adler said.

"And your damned opinion ain't worth shit, Gus. I got a job for you."

"A gun job?"

"Maybe. I want you to ride out to Jethro Swain's house, you know where he lives, and see if that Slocum feller shows up there."

"The one whose face is on the dodger?"

"That very one."

"And if he shows up?"

"Kill him," Scroggs said.

Adler grinned. There was a salacious sparkle in his eyes as if he had swallowed a tankard of ale laced with rotgut whiskey. He rubbed his hands together and then touched the grips of his pistols.

"Now you're talkin', Willie."

"Slocum has killed two of my men already, Gus. You mind your P's and Q's or you'll decorate a grave of your own."

"Haw. That ain't likely."

"Bring me the bastard's head, Gus."

"Hell, I'll bring you his corpse, Willie. That be good enough?"

"Just so's it's full of bullet holes."

Adler grinned. He turned on his heel and walked up the stairs, the clump of his boots resounding in the hollow confines of the basement.

He rode westward with the dawn, the sun at his back, streaming rivers of light in front of him, gilding the rocks and plants with soft flames that burned up the night dew that sparkled like tiny jewels on cactus flowers and minute grains of sand.

19

Penelope stepped out the back door of the adobe and waved to her uncle and Slocum. She wore a wan smile on her face, and there were dark smudges under her eyes. She looked haggard, as if she had not slept, and if she had, she had slept in her clothes. Her dress was wrinkled and shapeless against the curvaceous shape of her slender body.

Obie waved at her. She held up a hand in greeting as if she did not have the energy to wave back.

Slocum and Swain stopped next to the stables, where Juan Gomez was waiting, his rifle draped across one arm, his hand on the stock. The two men dismounted, handed their reins to Carlos.

"We ain't stayin', Carlos," Swain said. "Just hold on to our horses for us."

Just then, they all heard a man's voice calling out Penny's name. Swain recognized the voice. It was Jethro's and came from inside the house.

He looked at the back door, but Penny was gone. The doorway was empty. Swain frowned.

"I think there is someone who watches the house," Juan said.

Swain turned and looked at him.

"What makes you say that, Juan?" he asked.

"I see something in the east. I did not know what it was. I tell Carlos to look. He says he see it, too."

"What was it?" Swain's brow was wrinkled in concern, his forehead lined with furrows as he squinted to block the rising sun.

"I do not know. It is just a small speck. Very far away. But it moved. I see it. Carlos sees it. Then it is gone."

"A horse? A rider?"

"Maybe," Juan said. "I look all around, but I do not see nobody."

"Maybe we'd better take a look for ourselves," Slocum said. "Whatever it was, it was coming from Socorro."

"I'm going to check on Jethro first," Swain said. "Juan, you keep your eyes peeled. You see anybody out there, you let me know."

Juan nodded in assent.

Carlos spoke up when he thought Swain was going to walk away.

"I hear something," he said. "Ten, maybe fifteen minutes ago."

"What did you hear?" Swain asked.

Carlos pointed to a spot north of the stables.

"Out there. I hear a horse. I hear some animal or something making noise with the rocks."

"Like a horseshoe?" Swain asked.

"Maybe. I do not know. I look, but I do not see nothing."

"You boys keep lookin' and listenin'," Swain said. "I'm going to look in on my brother. You coming, John?"

Slocum followed Swain into the house. They both looked into the sick room, but the bed was empty.

"We're in here," Penny called, and they walked into the front room. Jethro was sitting up on the sofa. Penny sat beside him, taking his pulse.

"Hello, Jethro," Swain said. "You look like hell."

Jethro made a raspy noise in his throat. His mouth was open and his neck muscles were drawn taut.

"Pa, this is the man I told you about," Penny said as she removed her two fingers from Jethro's wrist. He's the man who saved you. His name is John Slocum."

"Slocum," Jethro said, drawing the name out in long string of vowels and consonants.

"Glad to see you're up out of that bed," Slocum said.

"Thank you, Slocum," Jethro said, and again, the words came out very slowly.

"You didn't unsaddle your horses, Uncle Obie," she said. "Does that mean you're not staying?" Penny patted her father's left hand in reassurance as she turned to her uncle.

"Me and John are going to ride up to my ranch pretty quick," he said.

"I don't think we ought to leave just yet, Obie," Slocum said. "You know why."

"Yeah, you may be right. We'll stay awhile, Penny," Swain said.

"What's John talking about, Obie?" A look of alarm spread across Penny's face as if there were cold ripples under her skin. She looked even more pale and wan as her eyes danced with light.

"Oh, nothing," Swain said. "The boys might have seen something. Or heard something. It's probably nothing. You had a good night? Quiet and all?"

"Yes, it was very quiet. Pa got restless toward morning. I

was up with him. He wanted to get out of bed and I gave him some warm goat's milk and he ate a piece of toast. He's still very weak, but his temperature is back to normal and his pulse is steady. He's just worn out, I suppose."

"I'm going back outside," Slocum said. "I might ride around and see if there's anything to what Juan and Carlos saw."

"Or heard," Swain said.

"Yeah. It never hurts to check."

"Be careful, John," Penny said.

"So long, Jethro," Slocum said. "I hope you get back on your feet."

"*Adios*, Slocum," Jethro said, and the words came out at a faster clip.

Slocum walked out the back door and headed for the stables. There was no sign of Juan, but Carlos was tying the reins of the horses to a corral pole.

He came within two paces of Carlos when he heard the rifle shot. It cracked like a bullwhip in the still air and Carlos crumpled to his knees. Blood spurted from a dark hole in his neck. He made a gurgling sound and clutched his throat. The reins dropped from his hand.

Slocum saw a shadow off to the south. The shadow became a running man. Sunlight glinted off the stock of the Henry rifle. Slocum recognized the weapon as an old Yellow Boy, .44-40.

He knelt down to see about Carlos.

Carlos tried to speak, but bubbles of blood came out of his mouth instead of words. His eyes went wide and wild as he gazed into the blue sky where his eternity lay.

Slocum crouched low and watched Carlos's eyes cloud over with the frost of death. He twitched once and then was still.

Juan emerged from behind the stable, a rifle raised to bring to his shoulder.

Slocum clawed for his dangling reins as Ferro turned in a hard tight circle.

"Do you see him, Juan?" Slocum called out.

"I see him. But he run away."

"I'll go after him. You keep watch here."

Slocum pulled on the reins and stopped Ferro's restless circling. He climbed into the saddle. From his vantage point, he saw a man mount a horse and then ride over a small rise, away from the house.

Swain ran out of the house, saw Carlos lying next to the corral, and yelled at Slocum. Slocum had Ferro in a gallop and did not hear Swain call out.

He headed for a puff of dust just beyond a sloping rise in the land. He loosened his rifle in its scabbard, but let it stay in the boot.

Just before topping the rise, Slocum turned Ferro and headed on a southward path. He would either cut off the bushwhacker's escape or be able to see him before the man could get off another shot.

He topped the rise and was dismayed to see no sign of the rider. Instead, there was a deep arroyo, signs of previous flash flooding, and the shooter had disappeared somewhere in the gully.

He reined up Ferro and came to a halt.

He cupped a hand to his ear and listened.

Nothing.

Not a sound. Not the scrape of an iron hoof on stone, nor the crunch of gravel or sand. Just the low keening of a northwesterly breeze. And nothing in sight but sagebrush and cactus, mute rocks, and miles of empty sandy land.

A slight shiver ran up Slocum's spine.

Whoever had shot Carlos probably meant to shoot *him*. He thought back. He was close to Carlos when the shot rang out. In fact, Carlos had been between him and the gunman. There was no reason to kill Carlos. But someone had a reason to kill Slocum.

And whoever it was, was damned smart and knew the lay of the land.

Slocum nudged Ferro with his blunt spurs and eased the horse into the shallow arroyo. He stared ahead, but also kept glancing up to the skyline. And he watched his backtrail, just in case the shooter meant to outfox him and come up from behind.

Then he heard a noise ahead of him.

Slocum drew his pistol.

A horse was galloping toward him. The sounds became louder and louder.

Slocum cocked the hammer back and waited, hunched over behind Ferro's neck like a crouching mountain lion.

20

The riderless horse, a sorrel gelding, rounded a slight bend in the arroyo and headed straight for Slocum. Its stirrups flapped like leather pennants, and its ears lay flat as if it were on the attack.

Just before the horse reached him, Slocum heard a loud long whistle. The horse skidded to a stop and wheeled in a tight circle, then raced back around the bend and disappeared from sight.

Slocum ducked just before he heard the resounding crack of a Henry rifle. The bullet made a whoosh just over his head. Atop the ridge, he saw a man rise from a prone position. Sunlight glinted golden off the Henry's receiver, shooting a blinding shaft of light straight into Slocum's eyes.

He pulled his pistol from its holster, but knew the man was out of range. It would even have been a tough rifle shot, because the man turned and ran and the split second of opportunity was gone.

Slocum marveled at the sorrel gelding. It was obviously well trained. It had performed its task like a circus animal. Which might mean that its owner was pretty smart, too.

And a crack shot. One second longer, had he been sitting tall in the saddle, he would have caught that .44-caliber bullet and lost part of his head, the part that saw and thought. It was a close call.

He turned Ferro and galloped out of the gully. He rounded the opening and rode up to the ridge. He was hunched low over the pommel of his saddle, just in case the rifleman was lying in wait farther along the ridge. He kept Ferro at a quick walk, and peered along his neck and mane, watching for any sudden movement, any sign of man or horse.

He heard the muffled sounds of hoofbeats, but couldn't locate where they were coming from, either at the far end of the ravine or somewhere beyond a rise up on the ridge. He peered down at the spot where the man had lain when he fired off that last shot, and saw where the ground had been disturbed by boot tracks and flattened by a man's weight between two clumps of sagebrush and Spanish bayonets. He followed the running tracks, his pistol at the ready, cocked and in his right hand.

He heard another whistle and then more hoofbeats. They came from the far end of the gully, where the sun gilded the rocks and splayed beams along a wide flat space where the ground had been ravaged by a violent flood sometime in the past year.

Off to the left of the flood plain there was a jumbled pile of rocks that formed a small hillock. Slocum headed for that spot, an idea forming in his mind. He rode up to it and then circled it. Then, he rode Ferro to a bowl-like depression some yards away. He dismounted and ground-tied the horse to a clump of sagebrush. He slipped his Winchester

'74 from its boot and walked back to the pile of rocks.

There, he set the rifle between two rocks, pointing it at the arroyo. He took off his hat and placed it on a higher pile just behind where he had placed his rifle. He drew his knife and cut some sagebrush, then carefully dragged it over his tracks leading away from the rock pile. He circled back to a low point in the land overlooking the rock pile and lay down in a narrow hollow overgrown with sagebrush and prickly pear cactus flanked by stands of yucca. He drew his pistol and lay with it in his outstretched hand. Sand and small pebbles burrowed into his legs and chest. He breathed the fine dust through his nostrils until the disturbed ground had settled.

He waited and he listened. He imagined himself as part of the landscape, lying perfectly still, much as a startled jackrabbit would hop to a large rock or clump of brush and freeze there, making itself virtually invisible.

Soon he heard the soft crunch of gravel with a slight ring to it. A horse, walking very slowly, somewhere down in the arroyo. He heard his own slow breathing, and he slowly eased the hammer back on his Colt, squeezing the trigger slightly to avoid the telltale click of the hammer cocking back. He relaxed his hand around the grip and let the pistol rest in the palm of his left hand.

A few moments later the sound of the horse ascending the slight slope leading from the gully grew louder.

Slocum waited and watched. He did not move his head or any part of his body.

The rider emerged from the arroyo. He and his horse moved with caution. The man slumped over his saddle horn, presenting a low silhouette. But Slocum could see him clearly. The man reached the plain and looked on both sides of his horse. He reined up and then sat up straight in the saddle.

Slocum, without moving his head, shifted his gaze to take in the pile of rocks, his stationary rifle, and his hat resting on a rock that filled its crown and was in no danger of blowing away with any sudden gust of breeze.

The man on the sorrel turned his head and surveyed the desolate land all around him.

As Slocum watched, the man slipped his Yellow Boy from its sheath and cocked it.

He rode closer to the rock pile, guiding his horse with his knees.

He halted the horse and brought the rifle to his shoulder. He bent his head and nestled his cheek against the stock, taking careful aim at the black hat Slocum had placed for a decoy.

The Yellow Boy spoke with a loud explosion. There was the crack of the bullet leaving the muzzle at a high rate of speed and then the whisper of its flight.

Slocum's hat flew in the air. Rocks crackled as they broke under the impact. Pieces of it sprayed out in a triangular arc, and the echo of the muzzle blast faded in the morning air.

The shooter kicked his spurs into his horse's flanks and laid the rifle across his lap. He headed straight for the pile of rocks. His path would take him within a few feet of where Slocum lay in hiding.

Slocum judged the distance and gauged the spot where he would make his move. The man did not look anywhere but straight ahead at the rocky hillock.

His mistake, Slocum thought.

When the rider came within a dozen feet of where Slocum lay, he slowly raised his gun hand and took aim at a point just behind the horse's right leg, just above its rib cage.

He held his breath, sighted down the barrel until the rear

sight was centered by the front blade. He squeezed the trigger. The pistol roared with the explosion and the recoil slammed the grip against the palm of Slocum's hand.

He scrambled to his feet. He holstered his gun and drew his knife as the horse staggered and its legs turned rubbery. Great gouts of red blood spurted from its wound and it staggered sideways before it fell in a heap. Its heavy body made a loud thud. The rider tumbled from the saddle and screamed when the horse's flank crashed down on his foot.

As Slocum rushed up and jumped over the horse, knife in hand, Adler pushed off the ground and stood up.

"Were you looking for me?" Slocum asked as he closed on Adler.

Adler's eyes were fixed on the knife in Slocum's hand and he drew his own.

"If you're Slocum," the man said with a snarl.

"I am," Slocum said and slashed at Adler's belly.

Adler backed up, the blade tip just barely missing him, and began to stalk Slocum in a tight small circle.

The two men, arms extended, flashed their knives and parried for position with empty slashes designed both to intimidate and keep the other at bay.

Slocum feinted to his right and Adler turned to meet the thrust that never came.

Instead, Slocum rushed to his left and kept running past Adler after leaving a gash in his shirt that drew blood from his flesh just above his belt line.

Adler did not cry out. He only grunted and steeled himself against the pain. He twisted to go after Slocum.

Slocum had not only flanked Adler, but circled to the man's left side and charged at him again. Adler turned to fend off the attack with Slocum's knife.

Slocum waved his knife, but he slammed a left hook into Adler's jaw that turned the man's head a good forty-five

degrees and made his eyes cross. A pale red stain appeared
on Adler's jaw and he shook off the shock of the sudden
pain and lashed out at the retreating Slocum with jabs and
wild arcs that fell short of their intended mark.

The sun glinted off Adler's blade, a large Bowie knife,
sharp as a surgeon's scalpel on both sides of the blade. It
was a formidable weapon, much larger than Slocum's blade,
but awkward to handle in a close knife fight.

"My horse you killed, Slocum," Adler snarled. "For that,
I kill you."

"Hated to shoot your horse," Slocum panted, out of
breath. "You deserved it more than he did."

"Son of a whore," Adler spat. Then he lunged at Slocum,
his blade drawn back waist-level so that he could thrust the
knife straight into Slocum's gut.

Slocum danced away, his belly drawn in.

Adler's momentum carried him a few feet past Slocum.
Adler stumbled to regain his footing and swing back around
for another parry. Slocum followed him and chopped Adler
in the back of his neck.

Adler staggered and his knees buckled. He turned and
sliced an uppercut with his knife.

Too late. Slocum drove in, avoiding the upthrust of Adler's
Bowie, and jabbed the man just above his belt buckle.

Slocum buried his knife to the hilt. Adler grunted and
bent over. Slocum twisted the knife and ripped a hole in the
outlaw's stomach. Slocum pushed downward as he withdrew his blade and the honed edge cut into a part of Adler's
intestine. A foul odor spewed from the wound in a gust of
steamy and putrid gas.

Adler gasped in pain. Blood and stomach matter seeped
through the hole in his belly. A blue coil of intestine pushed
through the slit and gave off a terrible stench.

"You swine," Adler hissed.

Slocum watched the man sway back and forth, his legs giving way beneath him as if they had turned to molten rubber.

"Ah, I die so slow," Adler breathed.

He collapsed to his knees just as Swain rode up at a gallop, his pistol in hand.

"That the man who killed Carlos?" he asked as he reined his horse to a stop.

Adler sank to his knees. His Bowie knife slipped from his grasp and he held his bleeding innards with both hands, a wild look in his eyes.

"Shoot me," Adler said. "I know I die."

"Way too sudden, stranger," Slocum said. "I want you to think about your miserable wasted life."

"I am Gustav Adler."

"I know who you are," Swain said.

"You used to be Gustav Adler," Slocum said. "Now, you're nothing but a piece of shit."

Adler's eyes flashed for one last time and then the blueness paled to a dull frost and there was a gurgle in his throat as he tried to speak, tried to draw in one more breath.

"He's finished," Swain said.

Adler crumpled and his body twitched a few times, and then was still.

"He who lives by the knife shall die by the knife," Slocum said. He wiped the bloody blade of his knife on his trousers and slipped it back in its sheath on the back of his belt. He drew his pistol, ejected the empty hull, and shoved a fresh cartridge into the cylinder.

"Too bad about his horse," Slocum said as he looked up at Swain. "I'd have liked to send his body back to town strapped across his saddle. That horse was well trained and he probably would have headed straight for the Socorro Saloon."

"Maybe Juan could pack his corpse back to Socorro and dump it right in front of the saloon."

"No," Slocum said. "I'll do it. I want a showdown with Scroggs and that bastard they call the Shadow. Otherwise, Scroggs won't quit."

"We'll skip goin' to my ranch," Swain said. "I'll go with you. Otherwise, it ain't goin' to stop. Scroggs won't never give up."

"When I see him, he'll give up something," Slocum said.

"Yeah? What's that?" Swain asked.

"His life," Slocum said.

21

Sombra waited for Linda to come home. When he saw her walk down the street, he sank deeper into the shadow of her adobe house with its flagstone patio, trellises dripping with honeysuckle and wisteria, the path to her doorway lined with pansies and buttercups. The fragrance assailed his nostrils, but he was in no mood for perfume.

All Morgan could think about was finding Slocum and putting him down with a well-placed bullet. Had he known he would lose two friends to Slocum, he would have drawn down on him when he shot Roger Degnan. He didn't know then, though, what he knew now—that Slocum was wanted for murder in Calhoun County, Georgia, and that he was one bad hombre with a price on his head.

He wanted to choke Linda for taking up with the bastard. She had spurned his advances and not even Loomis, Adler, or Thorson had been able to get anywhere with her. She obviously thought that she was too good for any of them. And as far as he knew, she hadn't taken up with anyone else in Socorro. Until Slocum showed up, the bastard.

Linda opened the gate and glanced at her flowers. She unlocked her front door. A black Labrador retriever bounded up to greet her, followed by a yellow cat with white blazes on its body. She leaned down and petted the dog.

"Hello, Pepe," she said, rubbing the dog's head. The cat rubbed against her legs and she stroked its head and back. "Little Sunkitty," she cooed. "Did you miss me?"

Behind her, the door burst open and Sombra pushed her toward the sofa in the front room.

"What in hell are you doing, Morgan?" she yelled as he stood over her in a menacing stance.

"Where's that bastard, Slocum?" he barked. "I know you were with him last night."

"That's none of your business," she said defiantly. "Get out of my house. Right now."

Sombra leaned down and slapped her hard across the face.

"Don't you give me no sass, you bitch," he said. "I want to know where Slocum is."

She touched a hand to the place where he had slapped her. Her cheek stung from the blow. There were tears welling up in her eyes as she winced from the sharp pain of Sombra's slap.

"I don't know where he is," she said. "And even if I did, I wouldn't tell you."

"You know where he was goin', though, don't you?"

He doubled up a fist and she cringed, expecting that he was going to strike her again.

"I don't know Mr. Slocum's business or his whereabouts," she said. She held up both arms to ward off any blow that might come from that doubled-up fist.

"You lyin' bitch. You know damned well where he is and where he's goin'. Where did you stay last night?"

"That's none of your business either, Morgan. Now get the hell out of here."

"Make me," he said.

She drew her legs up onto the couch and tucked herself into a ball. Her arms covered her face.

"Damn you," she said, and kicked at him with her left leg.

He grabbed her ankle and dragged her off the sofa. Then he kicked her in the side.

Linda writhed in pain and Sombra kicked her again, burying the toe of his boot in her side.

The tears came fast and sudden then. She uttered a short sharp cry of pain and began to sob.

"All right. You want to keep your damned secret, you're goin' to be mighty sorry, lady. I don't have time to mess with you. I'm takin' you to Scroggs and let him put the screws to you. You'll talk, damn you, and tell us where we can find Slocum."

"You can't make me," she sobbed.

Sombra reached down and grabbed her armpits. He jerked her to her feet and slapped her again.

"Bastard," she said, and spat in his face.

Sombra punched her in the belly and she crumpled. Then he dragged her out of the house and marched her down the street. Pepe growled at him, bared his fangs. Sombra kicked him in the snout and the dog whimpered, tucked its tail between its legs, and slunk away. The cat ran out of the room, his yellow hairs bristling on its humped back.

Fifteen minutes later, Sombra dragged Linda into the back door of the saloon and jerked her upstairs to Scroggs's office. He entered without knocking. Scroggs, in a conversation with Sheriff Paddy Degnan and his brother, Roger, looked up, startled.

"What do we have here?" Scroggs asked.

Sombra hurled Linda to the floor. She sprawled on the rug, in pain, weeping, bruises on her face.

"This bitch was with Slocum last night and she knows where he is. But she wouldn't tell me. I thought you could make her talk, Willie."

Scroggs arose from his chair behind his desk.

"I damned sure can make Linda talk," he said. He glanced at Degnan. "Opium does wonders, and we can pull out a few of them long fingernails."

He strode over to Linda and glared down at her.

"You been a damned thorn in my side for too long, Linda. If you know where Slocum is, you better tell me right now or there's goin' to be hell to pay."

"Fuck you, Willie," she said. "You miserable little bastard."

"I wouldn't take that from no woman," Degnan said. "What're you goin' to do with her, Willie?"

"Morg, you take her down to the basement. Wu Chen is lookin' for a guinea pig to puff on his opium pipes. If that don't work, I'll burn her some holes in her goddamned tits."

Linda glared at him, but there was a ball of fear in her stomach that was growing and scratching at her nerves like some eyeless beast. It hurt when she breathed and she wished she could cry out and bring John Slocum to rescue her. She knew she would be tortured, like poor old Jethro Swain, but this time it would be worse. All she could hope for was that they would eventually let her go and she could find John and he would exact revenge for what they did to her.

She vowed not to tell them a thing, no matter how much they hurt her.

And if they killed her, and Slocum found out about it, they would all pay dearly. With their lives.

She knew about the basement and the thought of it filled

her with dread. But no matter what they did to her, she would not betray Slocum. Never.

For Linda knew right then that she was in love with John Slocum.

Deeply in love.

22

Slocum stripped off Adler's gun belt, pistol, and knife. Swain grabbed the dead man's Henry and took it and the scabbard with him. Slocum tied a lariat to Adler's legs and, atop Ferro, dragged him down to the stables while Swain walked alongside. The corpse bounced and slid, rocks tearing at Adler's face and hands, ripping off skin and fracturing small bones.

Juan stepped into view. He held his rifle at the ready. He looked at the battered body of Adler and made no comment.

Penny came outside and walked to the stable. Slocum dismounted, lifted Adler's gun belt off his saddle horn, and stood there holding the belt in his left hand.

"Is that the man who killed Carlos?" she asked.

"Don't you recognize him?" her uncle asked. He leaned the Henry and scabbard against the sidewall of the stable.

"Gus?"

"Yeah," Swain said. "Gus Adler. He tried to kill John, but John outfoxed him."

She looked at Slocum with eyes filled with wonderment.

Who was this man, she asked herself. This tender, loving man who could kill so easily?

"Are you still going to your mine, Uncle Obie?"

"Plans have changed," he said. "Unless we stop Scroggs, he'll keep sending killers to find me, or you, or Jethro. He won't quit. John wants to put him down and stop all the attempts on our lives."

She walked over to Slocum and took the gun belt from him.

"I'll keep this for you," she said. "Unless you want to carry two more heavy pistols around with you."

"Why a man would want to pack two pistols is beyond me," Slocum said. "You only have to trust one good weapon."

"You should know," she said and grabbed the gun belt. The weight of it made her struggle to keep the holsters from hitting the ground. She lifted them up, the muscles in her arm undulating, the veins standing out under the strain.

Slocum sensed a hint of sarcasm in her tone. He wondered what he had done to offend her. But he handed her the gun belt, then turned to Juan.

"I killed Adler's horse, too, Juan. So there's a saddle, bridle, and saddlebags up yonder. I don't want them, but you might want to use them yourself, or sell them."

Juan looked at Swain.

"You can go look for that dead horse, Juan, carry back what you can salvage. But come back here and keep my brother and niece safe."

"I will do that," Juan said. "And I will bury Carlos."

"Penny, I'll look in on Jethro one more time before we head back into town."

"He finally ate some breakfast," she said. "And he is walking a little. But he hasn't been outside."

Swain turned to Slocum.

"You goin' to pack Adler on the back of your horse?" he asked.

"No, I'll strap him to Moses."

"That blind horse?"

"It might be the last ride for both of them," Slocum said.

Penny and Swain entered the house. Slocum put a halter on Moses and led him into the sunlight. The horse stood there, his head drooping, one hind foot cocked, its moth-eaten hide rippling under the onslaught of horseflies drinking his blood as streams left tracks on the horse's rump and sides.

"Juan, before you go," Slocum said, "help me hoist the body onto the blind horse and bring me some pieces of rope. Can you do that?"

Juan leaned his rifle against the building and went inside. He came back with several strands of manila rope and dropped them near Moses.

"You take his feet," Slocum said. "I'll lift his head and shoulders."

They draped Adler's body over the old horse's bare back. Moses did not protest, although he turned his head and sniffed the dead man before blowing steam and snot through his nostrils.

Slocum tied Adler's feet and hands together under Moses's belly. He pulled the ropes snug and rocked the body to see if it would stay on during the ride to town.

"That's fine, Juan," Slocum said. "Thanks. Good luck with the saddle and tack."

"Yes. I can use the saddle and the bridle."

Slocum pointed to the south.

"You'll find the dead horse straight up there," he said.

He watched Juan pick up his rifle and walk away. Then he went into the house, where he found Penny, Jethro, and Obie all sitting together at the dining table. They were drinking coffee and there was an empty cup and saucer on the table.

"Coffee, John, before you go?" Penny asked. She seemed distant to him, perhaps preoccupied, or carrying some resentment toward him. For some reason. Maybe she could smell Linda's perfume on him, her sweat, the musky scent of her sex.

"Thanks," he said, and sat down.

Penny poured coffee into his cup from a dented pot that had seen much wear.

Jethro and Obie looked at him as he took his first sip.

Slocum felt as if he was being examined for some unknown reason. The look on Penny's face told him that she was fighting back a jealous streak. No doubt she had quizzed Obie about where they both had stayed the night before, and he doubted if Obie had mentioned Linda. But he was sure that Penny was suspicious and just on the brink of asking him pointed questions about last night.

She said nothing for several moments. She just kept looking at Slocum. Obie cleared his throat and turned to his brother.

"You feeling more like your old self, Jethro?" Swain asked.

"Fair to middlin'," Jethro said. "Some things are still a little fuzzy."

"Did the opium get to you?"

"I reckon it did some."

"But he's coming out of that, too," Penny said, releasing her eyelock on Slocum. "He'll be good as new before you know it."

"I'm glad to hear that," Swain said. Then he turned to Slocum.

"Soon as you finish your coffee, I'll saddle up and we'll haul Adler to town and dump him in front of the saloon."

"No need for you to come, Obie," Slocum said. "I can handle it."

"You can't face Scroggs and his bunch all by yourself. Or are you just going to dump Adler's body and ride back out?"

"I'm not going to dump Adler outside the saloon," Slocum said. "I'm going to haul that old blind horse right into the saloon."

Penny looked shocked.

So did both Swains.

"That's suicide," Obie said.

"Shadow will kill you," Jethro said. "Or Sheriff Degnan, or that snot-nosed brother of his."

"And Willie's no tenderfoot with a gun either," Obie said.

"John, you can't go there all alone. You don't stand a chance against Willie and his men."

"It's my fight," Slocum said. "I don't want Obie getting mixed up in it."

"Well, I'm damned sure mixed up in it," Swain said. He pounded a fist on the table. "Look what they did to Jethro, and if you hadn't stopped Sombra and Roger, they might have kidnapped Penny or killed her."

Slocum swallowed the rest of the coffee in his cup. He stood up.

"Yes, they might have done that if I hadn't been here, Obie," Slocum said. "And God knows what devilment Adler was up to. I think he was sent here to kill me, and then he probably would have gone after you and the rest of your family. So, it's time for Willie Scroggs and his outlaw brethren to pay the piper. They'll be surprised to see me, maybe, and that's to my advantage. I've run into such men before. When it comes to a showdown, they're all the same, hotheaded and careless. But I don't want them to do anything to you, so stay out of it. This job is mine to do. Mine alone, and I lay claim to it."

"Jesus," Jethro said.

Penny's face drained all its color and turned the color of paste.

Obie reared back in his chair and just stared blankly at Slocum.

As Slocum started to walk out, Penny arose from her chair and ran up to him. She grabbed him about the waist and looked up into his eyes.

"John, please don't do this," she begged. "I—I care too much for you to risk your life this way."

"Penny, if I don't stop them now, you and your pa will always be in danger, and so will your uncle. Please. I've made up my mind."

"Oh, damn you," she said. "It's about some woman in town, isn't it? I can smell her scent all over you."

"It's about nobody but you and your family, Penny," he said. "And it's about me. When I see something is wrong, I try to fix it. If Scroggs isn't stopped now, he'll hound you all to your deaths."

He pushed her away and strode down the hall and out the door.

He picked up the rope to Moses's halter and climbed into the saddle.

"Come on, boy," he said to Ferro. "We're going to town."

The sun was high overhead and the land was lit up like some magic landscape, the colors all sharp and brilliant. Somewhere a quail piped, and doves flew past. He heard a crow call, and as he left the Swain house behind him, he saw a coyote and a roadrunner dash across the road, the roadrunner a feathered streak, the coyote a gray shadow slinking through the cactus and rocks like some stray dog.

Slocum had no plan, but he knew what he had to do.

And he knew he had to do it alone.

23

Linda screamed when Scroggs ripped her dress off, tearing it down the front so that her breasts and panties were exposed.

"Tie her to that straight chair, Morg," Scroggs ordered. "There's some rope in that wooden box over by the wall."

Sombra walked to the box and opened it. He pulled out a strand of manila cord, thick as his thumb, and carried it over to the chair where Linda sat, trembling. He grabbed her arms and roughly twisted her wrists in back of the chair and began to tie her hands together. He cut the rope so that he had another of equal length. Linda glared at Scroggs and twisted her wrists to put up some resistance. But Sombra squeezed her wrists together and pulled the rope so tight, it cut into her flesh.

She winced in pain, but did not cry out.

"Her feet, too," Scroggs said, "and take off them pretty shoes."

Sombra squatted down, removed Linda's shoes, and bound

her ankles together. He rubbed a hand across both breasts as he rose to his feet.

Two women sat on one of the cushions with a male companion. They passed the pipe connected to a single bowl of water that was the hookah and inhaled the fumes of opium. Their eyes floated dreamily in their sockets as Wu Chen looked on in approval.

In the shadows, leaning against the whitewashed wall next to an Oriental tapestry, stood Hiram Littlepage, the shadow of a smile playing on his thin lips. He knew Linda could not see him, had not seen him yet, and that was the way he wanted it. He had never liked his brother and he disliked his niece even more. She had always treated him with contempt, if not outright loathing, and he didn't care what Scroggs did to her. Her screams and her visible pain had no effect on him, just as the pain and anguish of others did not unsettle his mind or beget his compassion.

Sheriff Degnan watched as Scroggs puffed on his cigar until the tip glowed an angry orange and red.

Then, Scroggs stepped up to Linda and leaned down close to her face, so that they were eye to eye.

"One last chance, dearie," he said, his voice oily and nasty as slime oozing from an ugly metal pipe. "I want to know where Slocum is right now. Is he with Obadiah Swain? Is he at Jethro's? You tell me and all this will be over."

"I don't know where he is," Linda said.

"But if you did know, you would gladly tell me, isn't that so?"

"I wouldn't tell you shit," she said, and her eyes blazed in angry defiance.

A wry smile curled on Scroggs's lips and then his expression changed.

"You think you're a damned queen, don't you, Linda.

But you're nothing but a greedy whore, livin' off the backs of other gals. Well, it's about time you got what's comin' to you. You won't talk, maybe, but you'll scream, lady. You'll scream your damned lungs out."

He puffed once more on his cigar until the tip raged with flame, then stabbed Linda's left breast. Her skin sizzled as the hot cigar tip sucked up all the moisture and seared her tender flesh.

Linda screamed.

She kicked both legs, but the ropes only tightened around her ankles.

Scroggs buried the tip of his cigar on the nipple of the other breast. Linda screamed again. She writhed in her chair as the pain shot through her nerve cells and electrified her brain. Tears gushed from her eyes and streamed down her cheeks.

She moaned as the pain paralyzed her, robbed her of her senses.

Scroggs smiled.

"See how easy it is?" he said. "Fire is a wonderful thing. It can make you forget who you are. It can make you crawl and beg. It can eat you alive."

"You bastard," Linda said, her voice laden with hatred, with loathing.

"See? Fire can even make you talk."

"I hate you," she said.

"Just tell me what I want to know, Linda," Scroggs said. "Then it will all be over. You can walk out of here and go home to your dog and cat, your pretty flowers, and your shady patio."

"You go to hell, Willie," she said, biting off the pain that threatened to twist her into a knot.

Hiram strode into view as if he had been just a casual passerby.

"Hello, Linda," he said in his most sarcastic tone of voice. "Enjoying yourself? My, what pretty breasts you have and I'll bet there's a big secret under those thin little panties of yours."

"Hiram, you scum," she said.

"Do it again, Willie. Burn her tits. I like hearing the bitch scream."

Scroggs held out his cigar to Littlepage.

"Here, you burn her, Hiram," he said. "You might enjoy it."

"Thank you, sir," he said. He took the cigar and held it close to Linda's neck, so close that she could feel the heat of it on her skin. She tried to shrink away from her uncle, but she was trapped in that chair, roped and hogtied like a white-faced calf.

"I know you won't tell Willie what he wants to know, so I'll give you something that might loosen your tongue."

Littlepage jabbed the cigar tip onto Linda's throat and pressed hard. She gasped in pain and cried out in agony.

"Now?" Littlepage asked and jabbed her again on her lips. Tears streamed from Linda's eyes and she doubled up in pain as much as she could, drawing her knees up and straining against her bonds.

They all heard a yell from upstairs in the saloon.

Littlepage stepped away from Linda and handed Willie's cigar back to him.

"What's that?" Scroggs asked.

"It sounds like Roger," Degnan said.

"Roger? I thought he was laid up."

"He ain't hurt so bad," Degnan said. Then he looked up and yelled out. "Down here, Roger."

A moment later, Roger came bounding down the stairs, wide-eyed and flushed of face.

"He's a-comin', I think," he yelled. He had his pistol

strapped on and his side bulged with thick bandages under his shirt.

"Who's comin'?" Paddy demanded.

"That Slocum feller. I'm sure I seen him. He's on a black horse and he's pullin' an old swayback behind him, and . . . and . . ."

"And what?" Sombra asked, suddenly interested.

"It looks like a dead man," Roger said. "Fact is, I think it's . . ."

"Who?" Scroggs asked.

"It—It looks a lot like Gus. Only he's dead and all bunged up, like he was trampled or beat to death with a board or a damned rock."

"Well, get after him, Morg," Scroggs said. "Don't just stand there with your thumb up your butt. You, too, Paddy. Go on out there and shoot the bastard."

He paused as Sombra started for the stairs, followed by Sheriff Degnan.

"Shoot the bastard dead," Scroggs repeated.

Then they all heard it. Hoofbeats sounded on the saloon floor above them.

It sounded like a cavalry troop had entered the saloon. The thumps of iron-shod hooves pounded on the wooden floor that formed the basement ceiling.

"Shit," Sombra said as he drew his pistol.

Just then, Linda screamed.

It was not a scream of pain, but a cry for help.

"John, I'm down here!" she shouted, and everyone in the room froze and looked at her as if she were the Angel Gabriel and he had just blown his horn.

The horn that called all the living and the dead to judgment.

Sombra wheeled and cocked his six-gun. He took quick aim and fired at Linda.

She screamed again as the bullet smashed into her chest, right between her scarred breasts.

She slumped over as blood gushed from her wound and spilled out of her mouth. Her head fell over her chest and her hair hung in long lifeless strands.

The shot echoed in the room. The trio who were smoking opium looked for a place to hide.

Wu Chen ran to a corner and crouched there in fear.

Hiram swallowed hard and rested his palm on the grip of his sidearm.

Sombra clambered up the stairs, smoke curling from the muzzle of his pistol.

Right behind him came Paddy and Roger, both with guns drawn.

And then, there was only a silence from the saloon. No more hoofbeats. Nothing.

Nothing but that terrible silence that was as loud as a volcano's roar. That same silence that engulfs an abyss on the edge of eternity.

The silence of not knowing and not seeing.

Just an empty, ominous silence above the sounds of boots on the stairs.

24

Slocum rode slowly down the street toward the Socorro Saloon. Passersby and shopkeepers stared at the strange sight of a man in black clothes leading a blind horse with a badly battered dead man tied on the saddleless horse's back. Liquid Spanish phrases floated to Slocum's ears, whispers between startled women and exclamations of surprise from men with carts or on foot, packing homemade pottery and colorful blankets on their backs.

As he approached the saloon, he saw a familiar figure outside. The man stood there until Slocum drew close, staring at the dead body on the blind horse and at him.

Slocum switched the reins to his left hand, raised his right, and pointed his index finger at Roger Degnan. Then he flexed his thumb so that it came down like a pistol hammer.

Roger turned then, and ran into the saloon. Slocum noted that he was packing a sidearm and there was a bulge in his shirt on his right side.

Slocum rode up to the batwing doors and touched his blunt spurs to Ferro's flanks. He leaned to one side and pushed in on the left door. Ferro pushed through the doors and Moses followed. Their hooves resounded on the hardwood flooring, echoed throughout the saloon like drums in a hollow cave.

He heard Roger's footsteps sounding on distant stairs somewhere down a dark hallway.

Then, he heard a woman's scream, followed by a plea for help using his name.

Slocum knew who it was the moment he heard her voice crying out for him to come to her rescue.

His heart pumped fast as he rode toward the hallway. He reined up Ferro and dismounted. He dropped the halter rope and led Ferro back to the batwings and slapped him on the rump. Ferro pushed through the doors and stopped in the street. He turned his head to see if his master would follow him. But when Slocum didn't, the horse stood there and waited, looking at the people standing in shop doorways or in the middle of the street. All stared at the front of the saloon with startled looks on their faces.

Lamps still glowed on the wall behind the bar and in corners of the saloon. Sunlight streamed through the front windows, spraying the floor with a misty haze of gold. Dust motes danced in the rays like ghostly fireflies and the room settled into a deep stillness.

Slocum heard frantic voices from downstairs. Then there was another scream, followed by a single gunshot that seemed as final as a vault door slamming shut on a tomb.

There were no more screams.

The sound of the gunshot filtered up through the floor and he heard its echoes from somewhere below him.

Then he heard the ring and thud of boots on the stairs. Many boots, at least a half dozen. The sounds grew louder.

Slocum tiptoed toward Moses. He reached for the halter and turned the blind horse sideways so that the horse was now between him and the hallway. Moses drooped his head and stood like a statue, unmoving, giving Slocum cover, protection against gunfire from whomever came down the hallway and into the saloon.

He peered under the horse's neck and saw shadowy figures heading his way. The lamps in the hallway cast light on drawn pistols. The first man stopped just short of entering the main hall of the saloon and went into a fighting crouch.

"Slocum, you sonofabitch, you in there?" the man called out.

He recognized the voice. It was Sombra's voice. Two men crowded up behind Sombra. He saw the light glint off the bluing of their pistols.

"Yeah, Sombra, I'm here," Slocum replied. "Along with Adler. He's not breathing."

"Bastard," Sombra spat.

"Get him, Morg," Roger said.

"Blow the bastard to kingdom come," Sheriff Degnan said in a loud, throaty whisper.

"I'll get him," Roger said, and pushed past Sombra.

Once in the room, Roger halted and looked around.

"He's behind that old blind horse," he yelled. He raised his pistol and Slocum heard him cock the hammer. Roger took aim at Moses and pulled the trigger.

The bullet from his pistol slammed into Moses's neck. It sounded like a flat hand slapping a chunk of raw meet.

Moses staggered a step or two from the impact. Blood spurted from the wound as if the projectile had struck a major artery.

Slocum knew that Moses was mortally wounded and would go down. He backed away, crouched, and ran toward the end of the bar nearest the street. Roger fired at him, a quick shot at a running figure. The bullet whined as it struck a nail in the front of the bar and caromed off to shatter one of the front windows.

Slocum ducked behind the corner of the bar.

Sombra and Sheriff Degnan pushed Roger out of the way and stepped into the room, both hunched over and ready to shoot.

"So long, Roger," Slocum said in a loud voice. He squeezed the trigger of his Colt and saw Roger buckle as the bullet tore a hole at the base of the young man's throat.

Roger clutched at the wound and blood spurted into his palm and through his fingers. He made a gurgling sound and his legs collapsed beneath him. He dropped to his knees, flailing his gun in the air, gulping for a breath that would never come through the crimson lake of blood that now clogged his throat.

Sombra fired a shot at Slocum and the bullet gouged a furrow in the corner near Slocum's face. Splinters flew and the bullet passed into the wall, striking the adobe clay with a dull thud.

Roger folded up and fell face forward. His pistol fell from his limp hand and clattered on the floor.

Sheriff Degnan screamed in grief as he saw his brother twitch and heard the death rattle in the young man's throat.

He fired off a wild shot that struck the mirror behind the bar, shattering it into dozens of piece that shot sparkles of light on the back wall until they fell to the floor with a tinkling of glass shards.

Moses twisted in a half-circle. His forelegs bent and the horse dropped to its knees like some equine supplicant kneeling to pray. Then his rear end collapsed and the horse fell to its side. Blood from its neck ceased, but there was a pool of it soaking into the floor, bright as barn paint.

Degnan and Sombra, their attention diverted for that moment, watched the horse go down.

They both saw the grisly sight of Gustav Adler, still roped to the dead horse, lying in a grotesque heap, his battered and sightless eyes closed, his arms broken and hideously angled like scattered sticks of kindling.

Degnan's jaw hardened and lights flashed in his eyes as he turned his attention back to his dead brother and to Slocum.

"I'm gonna get the sonofabitch," Degnan said to Sombra.

Degnan charged out onto the saloon floor. He squeezed the trigger of his pistol and sent a shot flying over Slocum's head. He ran another three feet and fired his weapon again, blind to the danger, so angry about the killing of Roger that he abandoned all reason.

That was a fatal mistake.

Slocum shot Degnan between the eyes at six paces.

The back of the sheriff's skull fractured and exploded into a cloud of rosy spray, bits of skull bone, and grayish-blue brain matter. Some of Degnan's brains spattered on the front of Sombra's shirt. He brushed the gristly mass away with his left hand.

"You come on out, Slocum, where I can see you. I got a bullet in my gun with your fucking name on it."

"Funny," Slocum yelled back, "I got a .45 slug that says 'Sombra' on it."

"Fuck you, Slocum," Sombra shouted.

Sheriff Degnan made a noise in his throat as his pistol dropped from his hand and he collapsed into a pile of clothing, voiding his intestinal contents into his undershorts. His eyes locked open in a sightless stare. His mouth stood agape and a quiver of leftover nerve electricity rippled down his spine and prompted one leg to kick out then go still.

Sombra gauged the distance between him and Slocum, taking in the body of Sheriff Degnan. Then his gaze shifted to the dead horse and the body of Gus Adler.

Slocum could see only a portion of Sombra's body and the snout of the pistol in the gunman's hand. He had four bullets left in the cylinder of his .45. He also had his belly gun as a backup firearm if he ran out of cartridges in his Colt. But he doubted if it would come to that, and if it did, it would be at close quarters. He, too, looked over at Moses and then at Degnan. Both offered some cover if he made it either place and might draw Sombra out into the open.

For now, though, it was a standoff. Until Sombra made a move, neither man had the advantage. Both had some cover and both were just waiting for the other to make a false move.

There was a lighted oil lamp on the wall just to the right of the hallway. Its flame flickered enticingly as Slocum wondered if he might shoot down the lamp and cause Sombra to come out of hiding.

It was worth a try, he decided. But that would leave him only three bullets left and he didn't know where Scroggs was, nor how many more men were down in the basement.

"What's goin' on up there, Morg?" Scroggs shouted.

An answer to my question, Slocum thought.

The voice did not come from down in the basement, but from a room somewhere down the hall.

"I got Slocum where I want him," Sombra boasted. He turned his head to throw his voice down the hallway. "It won't be long now, Willie."

"Well, go on and kill the sonofabitch," Scroggs yelled. "Me'n Hiram are right behind you."

So, Slocum thought, two more men waited close by, down the hall. Linda's uncle and Scroggs.

He looked again at the lamp near the hallway.

Worth the chance? And another bullet?

Slocum thought so.

He swung his pistol to bear on the lamp's glowing glass chimney. He held his breath and squeezed the trigger. His Colt boomed and he saw the bullet shatter the glass, hurling flame, the burning wick, and shining pieces of glass upward and outward. The wick, still aflame, tumbled a few inches. Then its quivering flame began to eat at the wooden floor.

Sombra jumped back, then poked his head out to see what had been broken. He saw the shattered glass gleaming on the floor and the little flame streaking out from the wick in both directions.

"Shit," he muttered and turned to see if Slocum was still where he had last seen him.

"If my bullet doesn't find you, this saloon will be an inferno right quick," Slocum said.

He took off his hat and slid it atop the bar.

Sombra reacted to the move. He fired his pistol and the bullet dug a furrow in the bar top. The hat moved as if touched by a gust of wind.

Slocum stepped to the side of the V joint in the bar and fired at Sombra. As soon as the bullet was on its way, Slocum ran toward him in a zigzag pattern.

Two bullets left in the Colt.

Sombra stepped out of the hallway and tracked Slocum with the barrel of his pistol. He fired once and missed. Then he fired again and went back into a crouch.

Slocum swung his pistol to bear on Sombra and squeezed the trigger. Orange flame and brilliant white sparks flew from the muzzle in a stream of exploded and burning powder. The bullet caught Sombra near the bottom of his right lung, and the force blew him sideways just as he squeezed off another shot at Slocum.

The shot went wild, slamming into the ceiling above

Slocum's head. Chunks of wood and whitewash cascaded to the floor in an eerie cataract that splattered onto the body of the horse and the corpse of Adler.

Badly wounded, Sombra steadied himself as Slocum closed in on him, running now in a straight line.

"Ah," Sombra said, favoring his right side and leveling his pistol at Slocum.

Slocum squeezed off the last shot in his pistol. He aimed for Sombra's heart in the center of the man's chest.

The Colt boomed as the cartridge exploded in the firing chamber. A plume of flame and sparks flew from the barrel on the heels of the lead slug. *Whap!* The bullet from Slocum's gun smacked square into Sombra's chest and blood blossomed into a bright red flower on his chest. The bullet tore through his heart, smashing and shattering arteries, burning veins to a crisp, and ripping out ribs before shattering a portion of his spine and leaving a hole in Sombra's back the size of a small muskmelon.

Sombra's pistol slipped from jellied fingers and clattered onto the floor. He fell sideways in a dead swoon, his heart turned to a bloody pulp inside his splintered rib cage. He was dead before his body hit the floor, and no more of his blood pumped from the black hole in his chest.

"Did you get him, Morg?" Scroggs called from down the hall.

Slocum held his left hand over his mouth and answered.

"Yeah, Willie. I got him."

The fire from the burning wick continued to grow and devour wood. It spread in two directions, then went to the wall and crawled along the base of the adobe. It grew away from the wall and widened its circle.

Slocum opened the gate and began ejecting empty hulls from his pistol. They clanged when they bounced on the floor. He started to feed a fresh cartridge into the cylinder when he heard boots running toward him from down the hall. He shoved only one cartridge in, then pushed the cylinder back into place. He slid the pistol back in its holster and pulled his belly gun from behind his belt buckle.

Scroggs stopped when he saw the body of Sombra in front of him. He had his pistol in his hand.

Behind him came Hiram Littlepage, who was also carrying a pistol in his hand.

The flames from the broken lamp flared up and spread to Moses and shot around the horse's head and stalked Adler.

"Hello, Scroggs," Slocum said. "I've been waiting for you."

"What the hell," Scroggs said, then raised his pistol.

Slocum fired his Smith & Wesson .38 from four feet away. The bullet went through Scroggs's open mouth and smashed his spine in two, paralyzing him even before his heart stopped pumping.

Littlepage stepped toward Slocum, his gun arm raised. Before he could line up his sights, Slocum shot him in the belly.

The wounded man gasped and struggled to breathe.

"If Linda's dead," Slocum said, "you won't ever see her again. She'll be in heaven; you'll be in hell."

"Damn you, Slocum," Littlepage groaned as blood seeped through the hand that clutched his belly.

Slocum strode to the wounded man. He put the barrel of his belly gun to Littlepage's head, just in front of his right ear and squeezed the trigger. The Smith & Wesson belched flame and a fatal bullet. Littlepage dropped to the floor, dead as the proverbial doornail.

Slocum raced past the fallen man and found the room with the trapdoor open to the basement.

He bounded down the stairs and entered the lavishly furnished basement. The aroma of opium hung in the air.

He saw three people huddled against the far wall, and Wu Chen squatted down under a tapestry with a golden dragon sewn into the fabric.

Then he saw Linda slumped in the chair.

He ran to her and drew his knife. He cut her bonds and caught her before her body hit the floor. Her face was covered with drying blood and her beauty buried under that mask of death.

"You all better clear out of here if you don't want to be burned alive," Slocum said.

Smoke seeped through the ceiling. The women screamed and got up.

Slocum slung the body of Linda over his shoulder and took the stairs two at a time. He heard footsteps behind him, but did not stop to look back.

He carried Linda out through the batwings. The saloon was turning into an inferno. He saw crowds and clumps of people out in the street.

Then he saw Obadiah Swain riding through the throng on his horse. Swain waved at him.

Slocum draped Linda's body behind the cantle of his saddle and patted Ferro on the neck to keep the horse calm.

He shoved the belly gun back behind his belt buckle and then drew his Colt. He began to feed fresh cartridges into the empty chambers when Swain rode up. Slocum holstered his pistol.

"I told you to stay with your brother and Penny," Slocum said.

"I don't listen too good. Who all's inside the saloon?"

"All the ones I came after," Slocum said.

"You set the place on fire?"

"I did. It's what they call a Viking's funeral, Obie."

Flames began to break out the windows and soon they heard bullets exploding. The roof was on fire and some of the flames had spread to the unfinished hotel next to the saloon.

"I guess that's it, John," Swain said. "Is that Linda on your horse?"

"Sorry to say, it is. I figure Sombra killed her."

"Probably. Is he dead?"

"What do you think?" Slocum said.

"I still want to show you my mining operation and my smelter, John."

Slocum rubbed the stubble on his chin.

"First, a shave and a hot bath," he said.

"I wonder where we can buy a drink of that Kentucky bourbon now that the saloon is closin' up for good."

"I know where," Slocum said. "In my saddlebag."

He walked back to Ferro, full of sadness for Linda Littlepage. She had been too young to die, too beautiful.

A face in the crowd caught his eye. He had seen the women before, fleetingly, in the saloon.

The younger one, he did not know her name, held up her hand.

Miranda stood next to her daughter, staring at Slocum.

Maria Luisa Echeverria, with her arm raised, waved at Slocum.

She smiled at him. He touched a hand to his bare top-knot.

He smiled back at the pretty young woman.

Life goes on, he thought. There were still a few Sirens left in Socorro.

Watch for

SLOCUM'S BREAKOUT

393rd novel in the exciting SLOCUM series
from Jove

Coming in November!